Richard Pages

By L. R. Cerna y March

Bibliografische Informationen der Deutschen Nationalbibliothek:
Die Deutschen Nationalbibliothek verzeichnet diese Publikation
In der Deutschen Nationalbibliografie; detaillierte bibliografische
Daten sind im Internet über http://dnb.dnb.de abrufbar.

© 2016 L. R. Cerna y March
Herstellung und Verlag:
BoD – Books on Demand, Norderstedt

ISBN 978-3-7412-9005-3

Table of Contents

Chapter 1 Stella Schmitt   7

Chapter 2 Sarah Downing   17

Chapter 3 Monika Lachmann   28

Chapter 4 Fatema Dochta Zakariya   37

Chapter 5 Frederike Stechow   51

Chapter 6 Siloé Barré   62

Chapter 7 Katarina Ramakow   71

Epilog   78

Chapter 1

Stella Schmitt

The new main railway station of Heidelberg was a through station, unlike the first station, a terminus station from 1840. The new one was located one kilometer to the west of the old one. At the time I arrived to Heidelberg on Sunday, 28 October 1973, the station was considered to be the most beautiful and architecturally interesting building of the German Railroad Company. At least, this was what the teacher had told us in 1972 at the time we had made a school excursion to Heidelberg.

Now in 1973 I had an admission to the university and had to register next day, Monday, 29 October. Until I got my room in the dormitories at Klausenpfad, I presently had to find the place where I was going to stay, i.e. a kind of 'bed and breakfast room' in Bergheim within walking distance from the station, easy to find, close to St Albert's church.

After registration at the Old University, located at the east side of the University Square with the fountain, I had to look for information, buy a students' card for public transportation in Heidelberg, check in Alfred Weber Institut, go back to Neue Uni, find the different locations and explore all other places before going to Klausenpfad.

Registration on 29 October at the Old University took about 2 hours and everything went smoothly. At information I got hand-outs with the necessary data concerning the students' life: places to eat downtown with coupons, meeting point called Kakaobunker, located under the main entrance of the New University, institutes and offices of public transportations.

I had lunch at the main mensa, a kind of students' dining hall, and former stable, and after getting the month ticket for public transportation, I visited the Kakaobunker at the cellar with the taste of a shelter under the New University. It had two access ways from the main entrance with its famous inscription 'to the living Spirit' above, either right hand to the main stairs at the west side or left hand to the other stairs at the east side of the building where I had an opportunity to talk about anything to many unknown people. The Kakaobunker consisted of one large corridor with wardrobe and a row of a few rectangular tables leading to the main room with square tables, a counter, a short corridor with access to the counter and to the east stairs with exit to the teachers' parking and a second room at the end of the building. People had access from both rooms to the counter which obviously was open to both sides. The meeting point was equally for teachers and students and had a chronical chairs' deficit. You get a chair and the world is alright. I bought a cup of coffee at the counter and looked for a seat. My first neighbor was Aurelia Sommer, a German teacher at the Interpreters' Institute; she was a strong-bodied, 164cm high and 58kg heavy person with short black hair and blue eyes. Her face was round, her profile convex; she had a finely chiselled mouth, a nice up-standing Bavarian chest and she gave me the impression to think first before talking, and her boyfriend Anton Tiede. Anton was a medical student; a meager-bodied, 182cm high and 72kg heavy person with black hair and black eyes. His face was oval, his profile plane and seemed to be always in a positive minded mood with his clear tenor voice. He gave me the first quick instructions for easy navigating in Heidelberg:

- "Did you arrive to Heidelberg by train?" he asked passing me the sugar

- "Yes and I have a room in Bergheim not far away from St. Albert's, later I will move to Klausenpfad" I said while putting a spoonful of sugar in my coffee

- "I see. You arrived to the train station and walked the Mittermaier Street until the corner Bergheimer Street, didn't you?" he said while someone asked for the sugar and we passed it to him.

- "Indeed, that's the way I came!" I said after making place for somebody at my left

- "Well, think now you are at the corner. By the way, your institute is located at the same corner, just crossing the street. If you look to the left, the street takes you to the freeway Heidelberg-Mannheim. If you look straight, the street takes you to the Walzbrücke, and Berliner Street. If you look to the right, the street takes you to downtown, at the left side between Bergheim and Neckar you find most institutes, hospitals, etc. of the faculty of medicine, then you arrive to Bismarck square with Horten and Woolworth, crossing the square you arrive to Haupt Street. The Haupt Street ends at Karlstor via University Square. You can take the streetcar for doing this too. You find left and right of the Haupt Street most of the institutes and class rooms of the university. At the

University Square you find Alte and Neue Uni with the big lecture rooms and our beloved Kakaobunker. At the other side of the street you find the famous library of the university. At Kornmarkt you find the Heiliggeistkirche and have a wonderful view to the castle" he said while making place for somebody to occupy behind him a free seat at the next table

- "What about going to Klausenpfad?" I asked him in that vivid environment

- "For Klausenpfad you cross the Walzbrücke, walk the Berliner Street until you reach Bunsen High School or take the streetcar until last station, i.e. Bunsen High School, and change to the bus to "Schwimmbad". I think this may help you navigating in Heidelberg the next days without consulting the city map", once again somebody was asking for the sugar

- "Wow, this was a concise and exhaustive instruction; easy to keep in mind too. Thank you very much, Anton" I said while passing the sugar to the next table

- "Don't mention it!" he said satisfied to have helped.

They also told me that only the main mensa had open for dinner. The other two in downtown were only for lunch, i.e Haus der Begegnung at Merian Street, not far away from the Studenten Karzer, and Collegium Academicum at Seminar Street. The best mensa was the one of the PH, and there was also another mensa at Klausenpfad, good for me to know this because it was going to be my residence during the first semesters in Heidelberg. Before leaving, we appointed us for the following day after lunch.

In the afternoon, I went to Klausenpfad to register for my room. As Anton already said, I had to take the streetcar and change to the bus at the last station called Bunsen-Gymnasium, that means Bunsen High School. The bus went via Zoo to Schwimmbad and I had to get out at the station before Schwimmbad. The complex consisted of a big parking, three high buildings, dormitory I, II and III, and a flat one with the mensa and a groceries' store in underground, a big hall and the Studienkolleg on the ground floor and two dormitory levels on top. My room was located at dormitory I, second floor, which means the one closer to the parking and bus station. Everything went alright and I had confirmation I could move in on Wednesday, 31 October.

Before going to my room in Bergheim, I visited the Alfred Weber Institut to get the latest information before the semester started.

Next day, 30 October, I met Aurelia and Anton at Kakaobunker and we spent a few hours with some other friends of theirs, that is to say:

Stella Schmitt, an advanced student of pharmacology, a fine-bodied, 166cm high and 58kg heavy person with blond hair and blue eyes. Her face was oval, her profile plane; she had a seducing mouth, a talkative tongue and a clear intellect and last, but not least a beautiful heavy breast.

Sarah Downing, a student of political economy, a fine-bodied, 176cm high and 68kg heavy person with dark-blond hair and blue eyes. Her face was long, her profile concave; she had a sweet fine mouth, an insubordinate tongue and also an attractive Scottish accent.

Henning Koller, another student of law, a strong-bodied, 174cm high and 73kg heavy person with black hair and brown eyes. His face was long, his profile convex and he had a smart look.

Monika Lachmann, a student of political economy, a fine-bodied, 156cm high and 53kg heavy person with brown hair and beautiful blue eyes. Her face was square, her profile plane; she had a North-German mouth and accent, light understanding and also a charming speech.

Fatema Dochta Zakariya, another student of political economy, a fine-bodied, 164cm high and 52kg heavy person with black hair and dark eyes. Her face was heart, her profile plane; she had rosy lips, beautiful accent, a clear brain and also an attractive and sunny nature.

Frederike Stechow, a student of law, a fine-bodied, 166cm high and 54kg heavy person with blond hair and blue eyes. Her face was heart, her profile convex-concave; she had a sweet mouth, a friendly manner and a nice voice.

Siloé Barré, a student of political economy, a fine-bodied, 162cm high and 50kg heavy person with dark hair and blue eyes. Her face was diamond, her profile plane; she had a delirious mouth, a nice French accent and also an attractive nature.

And Katarina Ramakow, a student of languages, a fine-bodied, 160cm high and 50kg heavy person with blond hair and blue eyes. Her face was triangle, her profile convex; she had a Polish mouth with the corresponding accent, a keen mind and also an attractive look.

This was later going to become our club.

The meetings became almost a ceremony for all of us and our relations improved greatly. We used to move sometimes to the inside patio in front of the Hexenturm or to the large stone bench between main entrance of the university and parking. We also got knowledge of some unique types around, like the English teacher Rudy at the Interpreters' Institute, a typical playboy with his collection of red-hair-ladies, the never-do-well Erasmo and the ambulant vendor Martin with all his magazines.

We started meeting on weekends at different places, mostly at Anton's and Henning's place because they had more room. Later in summer, we also did some excursions together and affinities frequently came out. My first excursion with the group was the Philosophenweg, Philosophers' Path, Way or Walk, the former Linsenbühlerweg, a simple path through the vineyards in the 17th and 18th centuries, became the Philosophenweg in the late Romantic period. While walking the way, Aurelia explained the name.

- "Richard, do you know the origin of the name?" she asked pointing at the sign with the name 'Philosophenweg'

- "Well, if you ask me that I am sure the obvious answer won't be the right one!" I answered trying to look smart

- "Indeed, some people say the change of name may be traced to the fact that Heidelberg's university professors and philosophers, like Hölderlin or Eichendorff, found this path a congenial place where they could talk seriously and contemplate while enjoying the charming view of the Neckar. On the other hand, some others say that in the 19th century the words "student" and "philosopher" were synonymous due to the fact that students had to start studying philosophy before beginning their proper studies" she finished ex cathedra

- "I see, the time of the seven liberal arts" I said feeling smart

- "Liberal is the right word for couples using the path at that time for twosomeness, etc." Anton said looking very innocent

- "That figures to you, Anton!" Aurelia added with a light disgusted tone

Aurelia was a nice German teacher with an additional job as supervisor of a rooming house for students at Haupt Street 240, where Fatema, Siloé and Sarah lived. In Sarah's terminology in university context, dormitories and rooming houses were halls of residence or simply halls.

The scenic route 'Philosophenweg' was established in 1817. We continued walking and talking and discovering postcard views of Heidelberg, fantastic views across the Neckar to the Castle, as well as memorial stones referring for instance to Eichendorff; a sandstone stele with a poet's bronze or the Merian-Kanzel, a sandstone platform from where in 1620 Matthäus Merian certainly immortalized Heidelberg in an engraving, or the Hölderlin area at the eastern end of the Philosophenweg which was dedicated to the poet Hölderlin.

The walking also offered areas of colourful gardens, and spots with unusual plants and trees. The unique site and the warm climate of the city made many sub-tropical plants flourish along the walk. One could see there yucca trees, Japanese cherry, Spanish broom, Portuguese cherry, lemon, rhododendrons, cypresses, pomegranate, gingko, bamboos, pines, palms, almond trees and, and, and... Everything blooms weeks earlier in that corner.

After having done the 2 kilometers of the walk forth and back, we decided to continue hiking to the top of the hill, called Heiligenberg, visited the ruins of the churches and the Thingstätte, ate a sausage with chips at the service area and took the bus back to town. This was a tour we all liked very much and did walk many times.

One day I was second at Kakaobunker and wondered about Sarah's doing and she explained to me that she had to check her sugar values frequently due to her diabetes. Then Anton and Henning came in and started a very interesting introductory lecture about diabetes, toxicology and forensics. Main message was, that by diabetic patients there is always a credible explanation for shot traces and that some injected toxic substances are not easy to detect in forensics if the coroner doesn't know what to specifically look for, unlike swallowed pills easy to find as left-over in the victims' stomach. Meanwhile all club members were present and we started suggesting some activities we could do together.

For the following semester, Henning suggested we could do some sports at the Sports Institute of the university. Within the frame of "General Studies" the university offered some sports to all students. We decided to register for table tennis and sauna if the timetable fitted to ours. Henning got the details and we decided to register for table tennis on Wednesdays 17:00-18:30h and sauna on 19:00-19:45h.

Except for Aurelia and Stella, the ladies of our group were all diabetic and had to make sure to check this point with their doctors. Since there were no objections we proceeded as suggested, and observing the precautions the doctors had specified, like having time after time an 'emergency snack' in the pocket.

The Sports Institute was sited adjacently to the dormitories in Klausenpfad. That's why I suggested, after sports, to walk to my place and have 'Brotzeit', our dinner, in there. We could use the floor kitchen or go to the top floor of my building and use the 'social rooms' up there and later have a drink in one of the bars I, II or III in the corresponding cellars. The bus to town departed daily at 21:15h, 21:45h, 22:15h and 22:45h. The last bus left daily at 23:15h.

Some times during our 'Brotzeit' the ladies checked their sugar values and when necessary they injected themselves their treatment or we, Aurelia, Stella, Henning, Anton or me, did it for them. After a while we were all experts in injecting insulin.

Stella frequently stayed overnight at my place.

The moments with Stella were a new experience for me. None of my words meant I wished females to tell me the way I should go. Until then, I'd run away when some good willed person spontaneously attempted to convince me to follow his or her advice. No matter if it was supposed to be good for me. Like a snail, I coiled back in my shell and have had it my way, for my best or my worst... I never gave time to time but kept going ahead. A sheer chance catapulted me into the world of poisons by means of the first woman I could accept, maybe because she never intended to possess me. It was my second winter in Heidelberg and I had just commenced in summer that unique relationship with Stella. We were the best adult team one can imagine.

One evening, sitting on the large stone bench in front of the main entrance of our university, we were eating our sandwiches, talking about Anton's and Henning's opinion about undiscovered murders, and after discussing whom we wanted to kill most she said:

- "The point is not to kill somebody, but to commit a perfect crime with an unsuspicious tool. My uncle brought from overseas a bunch of exotic crops from which I organized some that I would like to transform in highly toxic substances"

And I replied:

- "It sounds risky and interesting for people with insane imagination"

We kept talking about the crops and about all she knew about them and that she needed an aid to assist her in the experiments. She asked me to be her assistant and a refusal would have been out of the question. The feeling of connivance was stimulating for a boy like me at that time. It was like having the first shot for an addict. It was 22:00h as we left the university with the famous inscription. That night I didn't sleep a single second at all due to my excitement and to the fact that we were trying to find good time windows for the time we were going to be working together. Her apartment was going to become our laboratory and we were going to need a lot of implements.

The workshops were slow and grinding since we didn't have time to work more than a few hours every second day; it was as good as a complete master's training in a chemistry school. Besides, we had to prepare and carefully schedule every next session.

First of all we had to catalogue her uncle's various crops she had managed to organize. We had barks of Strychnos toxifera,

Curarea toxicofera, Curarea tecunarum, Strychnos guianensis, Chondrodendron tomentosum and Sciadotenia toxifera, some kinds of Telitoxicum, Abuta and Caryomene, some snake venom, and some extract of venomous ants. This was a very hard job for a botanic and animal toxin ignorant like I was. I preferred catching frogs, giving them the injections, and counting the number of leaps frogs would take after being pricked.

Then, we proceeded step by step, i.e. we prepared a concentrate separately from each bark specimen: boiling the items in water for 48 hours, later straining and evaporating the concentrates until each of them became a heavy, viscid and dark paste, which we first didn't dare to taste because we didn't know if the paste had harmful effects if orally ingested. Later we learned the poison must get into the blood system to affect the neuromuscular transmission and it doesn't hurt to eat something killed by this poison. Well, all the pastes had a very bitter taste as we found out later. It was our first step towards our curare production.

At that level, the toxic potency was not strong enough for large mammals. The aim was to reduce its volume, improve toxicity and therefore the handling.

According to secondary literature, coroners can detect curare only if they search for it. That means, if at first sight the context is unsuspicious nobody will look for it; and that had to be proved.

Some months later, we obtained a blend paste with a toxic index of 1g per 10kg of human body weight. That meant, for a normal human of 80kg we needed to inject 8g of the paste, still much too much! Imperative for a lethal effect is that the toxic concentration in one single exposure must be sufficient to cause the desired toxicity; otherwise, the victims recover and have no ill effects.

Some hundred tests and frogs later, we obtained a blend paste with a toxic index of 0.2g per 10kg of human body weight meaning that for a normal human of 80kg we only needed to inject 1.6g of the paste. That is to say, the paste could unsuspicious be given in a shot of 3cc. Due to the quantity of paste we had, we were able to fill 32 shots in original insulin cartridges.

That was my introduction to the world of science! We were on our own.

In July 1975 we were ready for some field tests, but how and where to find appropriate candidates? We frankly couldn't advertise in the papers for this... But nerve and humor took us a long way.

We finally decided to risk something. The insulin-dependent candidates were to be called "cats" and the action was going to be "a visit to the veterinary". We thought that the only way to find the appropriate candidate and then remove the corpus delicti from the crime scene in due time was having a tight contact to the 'cat'.

Being in the good books of the other, money was not mentioned at any point in the proceedings.

We put together all the money we had and Stella left by car to Costa Brava with 3 shots disguised as insulin cartridges. She drove a blue Opel Kapitän she used to call "Old Henry" and we had a last talk before she departed:

- "I suggest contact channel would be preferentially snail mail" she said

- "Good idea, we write all messages in neutral language and short" I confirmed

- "And we do the final evaluation after my return to Germany. You stay home in case something should go wrong" she said pressing my hand

- "I stay home, but actually have no idea of what to do in such a case" I said looking ignorant

- "I keep you posted" she said and left with a smile on her lips.

Hoping to find one suitable test subject among the tourist centers, Stella decided on 29 July to stay in Lloret de Mar where she worked hard during the first days to get the necessary connections.

Once she found an adequate group, she had to select the potential candidate. Finally, she met an insulin-dependent cat, matching for the visit to the veterinary: male, 26 years, 169cm high, weighing 59kg, diabetic as she told me on the phone.

The replacement of the original insulin cartridge worked perfectly at the night Stella decided to proceed. It was Saturday, 9 August. She managed to leave his place with the empty injection and a good alibi: leaving at his side the empty syringe he had previously used as being the one he used for his last shot.

Next day, the news of the cat's departure reached very fast every one of the group. Everything went on as predicted. Registered cause of death was heart failure.

Stella gave me the short version of the test on the phone and asked:

- "Should I carry out a second test?" with great expectation

- "I think so, but in a different place" I said trying to reduce her enthusiasm.

We finally decided to make one more test in a different place, this time in Barcelona.

3 days later, it was once again easy for a lovely and charming girl like Stella to establish contact to a similar group and do the same procedure as last time. On 18 August she found the right candidate.

The "cat" was this time 27 years, 168cm, weighing 56kg, and diabetic. The physician didn't consider necessary to order an autopsy, and the death certificate was issued automatically with no problem.

Stella gave me a call again and we decided to put an end to the tests:

- "I send you all files and the last cartridge via snail mail and I leave Barcelona tonight" she said categorically
- "Which way will you take?" I asked
- "I'll take the road N11 from Barcelona to the French border" she answered in an easy mood
- "Alright, I'll be waiting for you, have a pleasant drive back" I finished in the same easy mood.

She departed in the same night of this 19 August in order to arrive next morning to Heidelberg.

I stayed in her place overnight waiting for her. On August 20, at 8 o'clock, the phone rang and I got a message from the Avignon police: Stella had died after her car careered off a road and crashed into a tree. The accident had happened on the road N86 at 02:34h that Wednesday morning and her close family had to be informed. According to the police, Stella arrived to the border via N11, took the N9 to Béziers, from Béziers to Nîmes the N113 and from there the N86 to Avignon, which she never reached. As I found out later, this was obviously the start of an endless bound of unexplained phenomenon that occurred to me. Based on statistics, there were an unusually high number of accidents and fatalities on this road before it was rebuilt years later and highway A9 was only partially inaugurated in 1975. At that moment I had to inform her parents in Zweibrücken, Rhineland-Palatinate, of the tragedy, take out quickly my belongings from her apartment and clear all traces of our previous work there in the past.

Stella's death left a bad taste in my mouth and left me with an empty wallet. I then decided to change my situation by means of rich females' inheritance to build bridges from my empty pockets to the future profit derived from my gold digger life. I still had some shots left...

Chapter 2

Sarah Downing

The news about Stella's death came as a shock to our group. No one could understand it and no one besides me knew the real reason for her trip to Spain. As all the ladies of the group were taking care of me, I had the opportunity to get more details of their financial situation. Monika, Fatema, Sarah, Frederike, Siloé and Katarina were all diabetics and potentially "cats". All of them were well situated, but for me Sarah was number one. Her parents had a battery factory in Scotland and some real estates.

After Sarah and I absolved the Vordiplom together, a kind of examination conferring an intermediate diploma, Sarah's father managed to find a six-week employment for us as trainees at a bank in Guernsey during the 76 SS vacations. It was a very instructive time and I learned a lot about offshore companies, also known as mail-drop corporations, phantom, letterbox, shell or brass plate companies and the special or privileged tax status of the islands in the United Kingdom. Such companies are the best weapon to cook accounts or to doctor balances.

I decided to deposit most of my salary in an account at the bank so I had already access to that world under student conditions. Sarah and I shared a bed and breakfast room in town and we had the possibility to have lunch and dinner at the bank. For the weekends we were on our own, of course.

Sarah's father invited me to stay one week after our trainee period at his house in Edinburgh. First thing I have learned was the correct pronunciation of the name of the town, so I did no mistake at the time we arrived.

Her parents fetched us at the airport and Sarah did the introduction:

- "Mum, Dad this is Richard Pages, my boyfriend" she said while kissing them on the cheek

- "Glad to meet you, Richard, I am Ann" she said and gave me her hand ladylike and with all options open

- "Enchanté, Ann!" I said and gave her the metaphoric kiss on the hand I didn't shake but just hold
- "Charmant, charmant..." Ann said with a benevolent smile on her face exchanging glances with her daughter
- "And I am Sean, welcome to Edinburgh Richard!" He said shaking my hand the Scottish way; well I supposed it was the Scottish way to squeeze the hand of the counterpart
- "Glad to meet you, Sean... Thank you very much for the invitation and warm welcome" I said while checking if all my fingers were still at the right place on my right hand

Ann was an attractive middle-aged fine-bodied, 174cm high and 64kg heavy lady with light-blond hair and blue eyes. Her face was long; her profile concave. She had a similar sweet fine mouth like Sarah and a similar voice. Sean was a strong-bodied, 174cm high and 73kg heavy male with red hair and blue eyes. His face was triangle, his profile concave and his hands were of iron. Sean took the lead to the car, a 73 Mercedes 280 and immediately began talking about the factory. The factory was sited between the airport and the city, at about halfway, in an industrial zone that looked as a poor forgotten spot of the past World War II. The production had steadily increased every year and the order books were doing well for the future. The soil of the factory had been completely contaminated with all kind of acids used in the production. However this pollution problem had been solved three years ago by means of a very happy and opportune insurance case and was not more a potential problem in case politicians would change their mind in matters of environmental policy. All in all, the factory yielded good profit and was an attractive investment object to whom it may concern.

Unlike the factory, their house was a very old and very nice one with all standards of the seventies. It was well located at Meadow Park with a nice garden and double garage, a natural stone house construction. It was a hipped roof house with some dormer windows and loft, first and ground floor, and a cellar. It had 4 bedrooms with walk-in closets and a home office room upstairs. On the ground floor the usual facilities with wardrobe closet, kitchen, dinner room, large studio and a large living room with chimney and porch to the backyard. The furnace or stove room was in the cellar under the kitchen and operated with the traditional fuel of the seventies. The ventilation was adequate and with enough supply of fresh combustion air. The fuel tanks were under the garage, and both units had the required fire resistant barrier between these two areas and the house. They also had there laundry and utility rooms, workshop, wine cellar and a bathroom. The house was equipped with real stairs and a lift.

After the short guided tour through the house, they immediately showed me my room and said we were going to meet in the living room half an hour later.

As I came in the living room they were waiting for me with full glasses and Sean said:

- "It is your first time in Edinburgh Richard, isn't?" He asked rocking back and forth in his iron hand a single malt bottle with an asking glance

- "That's correct Sean" I said nodding agreement

- "In this case we do some sightseeing in town. Due to the fact that today is Sunday, I suggest that we walk a little in town before tea time: Middle Meadow, Bedlam Theatre, Museum of Scotland, University of Edinburgh, South Bridge, Canongate, Royal Mile, until Palace of Holyroodhouse and then back the High Street until Edinburgh Castle. Close to the castle there is a nice tiny tearoom Sarah loves very much with delicious homemade cakes and sharing tables' policy where we can have a break" he said and gave me a glass with plenty of single malt Scotch whisky and we all touched our glasses

- "It sounds perfect to me", Sarah said after taking a sip from her glass

- "I knew you were going to say that" Ann added and took a gulp from her glass

- "Whatever you decide is alright for me" I said sniffing at my glass

- "Then we come back and have some dinner at home before doing the Murder and Mystery Tour at 21:30h, starting in front of the Witchery Restaurant in the Royal Mile" Sean said and took another gulp from his glass

- I thought: "What a delicious coincidence!" and took a sip from my glass

- "Monday is a bad day for tours, etc. so I suggest I show you the factory, Richard. The ladies can stay at home or come with us as they prefer" Sean said and sniffed at his glass in his best innocent manner

- "That will be great for me. I hope the ladies will accompany us" I said pretending to take another sip

- "Please Mum, say yes, please..." said Sarah soft giving up in her effort her soul

- "Alright, we go all together to visit the factory" Ann said and we all were glad to hear her saying that

- "Wow, what an exception, Ann visits the factory! I suppose it is because you gave her a good impression, Richard. Well, let's go for our walk!" Sean said and finished his glass and took the lead to the kitchen to put his empty glass on the pantry, what we all did after him like brave pupils.

The weather was exceptionally nice, so we left the house and did as suggested. Edinburgh was a nice town with a lot of hidden places, and almost each house in town had its own supranatural inhabitant as I was seriously told. In the past, the town was smoky, had narrow streets, countless 'wynds', and a smelly scent. At the time of my visit, it was all commercialized for the tourist industry.

The tearoom was a lovely place with eye-like windows, stroller parking at the left side of the entrance, delicious cakes and was run by a nice and very talkative family. If you managed to escape them, your neighbour caught you… They gave you the impression they were all intimate associates. Everybody had to play the game and enjoyed it.

On the way back we walked along the Parliament House and all the way down to the Middle Meadow and to their house again. Ann had already prepared a stew and she only had to put the Yorkshire pudding in the moulds and then in the oven for 20 minutes, while we helped her with peas and Sean looked for the adequate wine in the cellar. He returned with a Barolo red wine, well, 2 bottles, which we unanimously accepted.

Dinner was delicious, for British standards and the crème brûlée as sweet as necessary. After coffee, we made the kitchen clear and enjoyed our brandy in the living room. Ann and Sarah unsuccessfully pursued us with the scrabble.

- "Sarah told us you both have a nice group in Heidelberg" Sean said sniffing at his Cognac glass

- "Indeed! We kept in touch with them during our stay in Guernsey and Anton wrote he was going to finish his Physikum this week …" I said after taking a sip of the delicious Cognac Sean had served

- "What's that?" he asked with a vacant look

- "It is an intermediary preclinical examination for students of medicine" I explained

- "A medicine student, I see" Sean said looking into his empty glass

- "The group will wait until we come back to celebrate his completion together. As I understand, you also have something in your agenda you would be delighted to do in the near future" I asked with a malicious glance

- "Oh yes, we haven't had real vacations for years. Due to the factory we only have 2 weeks during Christmas, when we can close the factory with no great interruption of the production, so we dream of a 4-week car vacation through the United States" Ann shrieked out her words

- "You are the slave of the factory. By the way, at what time do we leave to the factory tomorrow?" I asked in my best businesslike tone

- "We can have breakfast at 7 and leave at 8" Sean added ignoring Ann's statement

- "That's perfect for me, what about you, addict ladies?" I asked the two scrabble ladies at the couch table

- "Breakfast at 7", Ann said in a military not ladylike tone
- "No problem for me" Sarah added in a ladylike tone
- "Ann, Sarah, Richard, I think it is time for us to get to the Murder and Mystery Tour at 21:30h" Sean rushed us

We left immediately after bringing the used glasses to the kitchen and arrived easy at 21:10h to the starting point in the Royal Mile. It was a nice 90-minute Scot tale for adults, and afterwards we were tired and went to bed fast.

Next day, the visit to the factory was very interesting and important for me. The soil of the factory was really clean and decontaminated. Considering the beautiful garden they had planted in there one could never imagine how ugly and insane it looked before. The plant consisted of 4 buildings, one for administration, one for production, one for magazine, tanks and ponds and one for garage and delivery. The skilled personnel was built by 40 blue collar workers, 2 janitors and door-keepers, 7 office employees and 10 drivers. Security and cleaning were outsourced. After lunch we concentrated on the accounting department, because the British way to make balances and accounts differed from the German way.

The knowledge I gained from these hours taught me the factory was a desirable gem for any investor. So I decided to continue my plan and talk with Sean about what Sarah and I had in mind. I first had to ask Sarah if she agreed on it, of course, which she did. That night we had a council with Sean after dinner:

- "Sean, Edinburgh offers foreign students the hands-on business administration in a two-semester course to make them job-ready on day one after studies. We would like to register for such a course next semester. In this case, we could stay here and gain the necessary skills to take care of the factory when you make next spring your highly desired vacation in the USA" I said after taking place on one of the comfortable armchairs with high sculpted back and ultra thin arms

- "That comes unexpected to me, but I think it is a good idea. I'll talk it over with Ann and I'll tell you our decision on Wednesday" Sean said looking to Ann who nodded her head in agreement
- "Wednesday will be alright for us, Dad" Sarah chuckled with a satisfied glance in her eyes
- "Same to me, Sean" I added with expectation in my brain
- "Tomorrow, we can do some shopping in the morning. I would like to show Richard the department store Jenners in the Princes Street and we'll have lunch in the Enchanted Platter" Ann said looking like a Sphinx
- "Enchanted Platter, Mum?" Sarah asked astonished
- "Enchanted Platter, Ann?" Sean repeated amazed
- "Yes! Enchanted Platter!" Ann said in her military not ladylike tone
- "I hope you will explain me what it is…" I whispered to Sarah
- "Wait and see!" Sarah whispered back.

Afterwards the ladies started playing scrabble and I went early to bed wondering about the Enchanted Platter.

Next morning, we had a lazy breakfast because Jenners didn't open before 9:00h. That time we walked Middle Meadow, Forrest Road, University, South and North Bridge and then turned left into the Princes Street. And finally, I saw Jenners, the oldest department store in Great Britain. Behind the Perfumes' Department we arrived to a huge and high oval hall, known as the grand hall, with three gallery floors and a gable roof with a lot of windows. In 1895, the year of the inauguration, the building was ahead of its time for Scotland. It had electrical light, lifts and air conditioning. First we walked around and I did a good job letting her believe I was happy to be put under its spell and admiring anything before we went shopping outfits, perfumes, after shave and all that jazz. At 11:00h we did a short break in the cafeteria while Ann called the Enchanted Platter for reservations at 12:30h. We continued shopping for one more hour and fortunately for me Jenners had home delivery.

From Jenners to the Enchanted Platter was a half walking on the way back home; we took The Mound down to George IV Bridge and there it was, the Enchanted Platter! The main entrance was at the level of the bridge on the second floor of the building, 80 m away from the Museum of Scotland in the Chambers Street. The third floor was a kind of panorama roof garden known as 'the terrace'.

We had a fantastic table on the terrace and an extraordinary polite service. We selected clams and Champagne for the beginning, and a saddle of lamb with baby fennel and aubergine and Bordeaux and water for the main course. For dessert we had the symphony with lemon and later coffee. Afterwards we decided to visit the museum and walk a little around before going home.

At home we prepared tea time with fresh scones and clotted cream, and the ladies started a new scrabble while waiting for Sean's return. He arrived short after that, so that the ladies were forced to cut their game. Before dinner Sean had still some work and calls to do and I was condemned to join the ladies to play.

For dinner we had that night cold cuts: sliced assorted salami, ham and a variety of cheeses, including some Cheddar. The bread was very British, but the coffee was alright.

After clearing the kitchen, men had no excuse and were condemned once again to play scrabble with the ladies.

On Wednesday, we prepared sandwiches to take away for lunch and did a large walk around town: Coronation Walk, Chalmers Street, Lady Lawson, Bread Street, Lothian House, Lothian Road, Hope Street, Albert Memorial, St. Bernard's Well, Darna Way, Gloucester Lane, India Street, Heriot Row, Dundonald Street, Great King Street until Alva Business Centre and Royal Circus. Then Frederick Street all the way down until Ross Open Air Theatre, Street Gardens, The Mound, National Gallery, Royal Mile, Old Fish Market, University of Edinburgh, Chambers Street, Forest Road, and finally Middle Meadow. All together 8 hours from 9 to 17 with two breaks.

Sean was already over as we returned; we were tired and happy to be back and had a lazy tea time and no scrabble.

That night we had a chicken dinner and council afterwards:
- "We think your suggestion concerning the two-semester course combined with our US tour is a good idea and completely agree with you" Ann said with a very pleased tone in her voice
- "Indeed, we both agree on it!" Sean confirmed with a slightly smile on his lips
- "Perfect! We check tomorrow the details at the university and keep you posted" Sarah said in a winner tone
- "I am quite sure that the course starts in November..." I assisted as Sean interrupted me:
- "Before you go into further considerations, we want you both to stay at our place and think you could have a paid part-time job at the factory, I think 10-20 hours per week would help you both, no hard working student should be stuck in the red" refilling my glass before we all touched our glasses to say good night.

Next morning, we went to the university to get the details of what we already knew: the course started in November and finished with an exam to obtain a certificate, recognized in Heidelberg. With the registration we could apply in Heidelberg for a 2-semester foreign study absence; this all being ruled in detail by the British and German academic exchange service. We did the registration the same morning because we coincidentally had at hand all required documents. Tuition had to be paid until 2 November.

Afterwards, we went to the factory and informed Sean. He immediately gave us the tuition money to be passed later to our accounts at the factory, gave instructions for our part-time work contracts, 15 hours per week, and to clear for me all legal requirements needed. After paying the fees we were all set, could prepare our return to Heidelberg and do some laundry before departing on Saturday.

In Heidelberg we had a lot to tell during Anton's party for his Physikum on Sunday and I asked him if he had some room for me to store a few things during my absence because I wanted to give up my room in Klausenpfad for the year in Edinburgh.

The institute gave us green light for the foreign study and also a recommendation letter. Everything worked as desired and we arrived again to Edinburgh the last week of October 1976.

Meanwhile, Ann and Sean had already checked the tour: 4 weeks in April, starting by car in New York and finishing in San Francisco via Colorado, Utah, New Mexico, and Arizona, approximately 3000-4000 miles. They enjoyed planning, so did I! During the first weeks I got somehow the overview of the financial circumstance of the family: Sean, Ann and Sarah were registered co-owners of the house and of the factory each to one-third. Sarah was going to receive before Christmas the power to act and sign on behalf of the firm and of her parents. I participated in most meetings with the lawyers, so I always knew what was going on. Studies developed well and the part-time job at the factory was very good for my pocket, although I had to invest some money in attentions to the tribe.

We spent Christmas together and had a good time, and no work at the factory for two weeks. University was, on the other hand, a hard job and we had to keep at it. The short and long of it is that we did a good job anywhere. From time to time we had dinner at Sean's golf club and had contact to his golf partners. I was a beginner in golf matters. Just the scrabble nights were for me not easy to take. In March 1977 we had the first examinations with good records, so Ann and Sean could leave in April with best and clear conscience to the US. On 3 April we took them to the airport and had lunch together in there before their departure. That night we did not play scrabble.

On 14 April 1977, we received a call at 18:00h, 10:00h local time, from Sheriff Marcos Corrales, San Juan, a county in New Mexico, with the bad news: they just had found the crashed car with

Ann and Sean inside. The rescue of the car was still in process, but the bodies were already recovered and in the pathology. Sarah agreed with the sheriff concerning the autopsy and we asked him for a funeral home in site to be contacted by ours in Edinburgh in matters of return transport of the bodies. We said we could arrive to New Mexico in two days, if we could get a visa for the States, and he gave us instructions to reach his place. Farmington was the largest city of his county and the Four Corners Regional Airport of Farmington could be reached by plane either from Albuquerque or Santa Fe, both New Mexico, or from La Plata County Airport in Durango, Colorado. The route Durango-Farmington could also be done in one hour by car; it was only 52 miles away. Jet aircrafts had landing problems in Four Corners because the airport was on top of a plateau with no possibility for extending the runways. The sheriff was going to fetch us at the airport. He made reservations for us in a nearby hotel as well as in a car rental office and also appointed a meeting with the funeral home. Confirmations were to be made next day, same time.

Sarah immediately called the golf club and asked whether the US Consul, one of Sean's golf partners, was there and requested him to wait for us in the club. We took our passports to the club, met him, explained him our problem and asked for help. Next morning we had our indefinitely valid B-2 visa at the factory, where we explained to the staff what had happened and what we were going to do next. Before leaving to the factory that morning, Sarah took from the 125,000 pounds in safe in the well hidden panic room an amount of 5,000 pounds in cash to be changed in dollars by one of the drivers. William Corner, Sean's substitute, was designated to take care of everything during our absence and also order on our behalf a funeral home in town to contact the funeral home in Farmington, as well as to carry out all formalities and prepare the funeral. Margot, the secretary booked for us a flight for next day via Durango and back one week later via Santa Fe, due to formalities to be done at the consulate before departure.

In this context I learned that each one of the family had a life insurance with a coverage amount of half a million pounds, death benefits tax-free at that time. Additionally, as Sean booked everything by means of his credit card, Sean and Ann also had extra risk insurance for 200,000 pounds and the rented car also had an insurance against all risks. We asked the lawyers to take care of all formalities and I decided to keep in mind the blessings of life insurance for later requests.

Marco was a very helpful sheriff in this matter and gave us 20 original death certificates as well as all information he had together with a copy of the file and medical report: the accident had happened on Tuesday, 12 April 1977, while Ann was driving on route 666 between Sheep Springs and Shiprock and suffered a heart attack. The coroner couldn't determine who died first. The car was completely destroyed and Ann and Sean had died instantly. Someone at the funeral home told us later that the route was known as Devil's Highway due to numerous accidents on that road.

The burial service took place in their parish church and the burial in Dean Cemetery, a privately owned cemetery sited between Dean Path and Queensferry Road. Newspapers published the obituary of their death and invitations were sent to relatives, friends, and employees to attend the funeral ceremony at the local church. After the burial, mourners were invited to the golf club for a buffet meal. Plenty of whisky and drinks were served. It was the Scottish after-funeral feast 'Dredgy'.

After closing that chapter with all formalities fulfilled we had to clear with the banks, lawyers and tax consultant the legal and tax points emerging for Sarah. And in this matter, we did not bark up the wrong tree with them. There were so many points to observe during the proceedings, like obtaining the right Grant of Confirmation, and properly using the 1975 Capital Transfer Tax, former Estate Duty, etc. The short and long of it was that Sarah didn't have to pay much tax and I got some valuable details concerning inheritance between married people in Scotland: upon death of one spouse, bequests to the other spouse do not incur inheritance tax and any intestate property by default will go to the spouse. In this context I registered Edinburgh as my main residence address. The move was certainly a feather in my hat.

Sean and Ann had a nice construction with mail-drop corporations and accounts with 3 millions pounds offshore in Guernsey, Isle of Man, Cayman, and Asia-Pacific. Sarah decided to keep the same construction but changed the currency into dollars under our both names and we planned to get married as quickly as possible. The 120,000 pounds left in cash and the 50 gold coins and jewelry we found later in the safe were of no public interest.

I gave Aurelia a call to keep the group posted about the news and also told her, Sarah and I were going to marry probably at the end of June, after completion of the course, and the group should consider coming to Edinburgh for a few days to celebrate the wedding with us.

We did the Schedule at the Registrar with plenty of time, so the minimum 15 days' notice was no problem at all. I also had a certificate of approval from the Home Secretary. At the same time we asked the golf club to rename our family membership. I was almost all set for the first shot.

After getting the certificate for the course, we married as planned on 28 June 1977, Tuesday, and celebrated the wedding with the group in Edinburgh. Our return to Heidelberg was scheduled for October and William Corner would manage the factory in our absence. I then also considered the options I had worked out for the factory: selling the factory to foreign investors or to the staff. In that case I had to find a way to get the necessary interim financing from the bank in order to allow the staff to buy the firm and to make mandatory for them to buy all participations back from deceased participants. Well, that was something they had to clear by themselves and at that stage not my business. I still had enough time because I wanted to keep the factory for a few years before doing the next step.

Speaking of next step, I had to clear the "cat" before August and make sure to have an alibi. I decided to give Sarah the shot the night I departed for a congress on Friday-Saturday, 29-30 July, 1977, changing syringes before leaving and making sure the shot had worked. She was going to be alone at home during the whole night letting the shot come into effect and was to be found next morning by the cleaning woman.

Following morning, the cleaning woman called me at the congress and gave me the bad news. I told her to call the doctor and wait until I came back. I gave the news to the funeral home and said the doctor was on his way; they should wait for the doctor at my house. The doctor arrived and examined Sarah's body and decided the cause of death was heart failure and signed the death certificate. Then the body was transported and prepared for cremation.

After the burial, same procedure as last time, I cleared all legal matters with the banks, lawyers and tax consultant and convoked a meeting in the factory to explain the options I had. They all agreed on the second option, accepted to observe strict confidence in the matter and 6 delegated persons of the staff had to find out which bank under which conditions would finance the transaction.

During the following years, the atmosphere in the factory was the better one can imagine and productivity steadily increased. After finding the proper bank and working out all formalities, the takeover was scheduled for November 1982.

At that moment I had a very gloomy picture of the situation because I was missing Stella.

Chapter 3

Monika Lachmann

The news about Sarah's death in July 1977 came again as a shock to the group. No one could believe it and no one besides me knew the real reason for her departure.

After putting my affairs in order I took my paraphernalia and returned to Heidelberg to finish my studies. Although due to the factory I had to frequently fly to Edinburgh. It was then 77/78 winter semester and my 9th semester.

In Heidelberg I rented a nice apartment close to the university where the group loved to make breaks. Once again, all the remaining ladies of the group were taking care of me. I selected Monika for obvious reasons as the next cat, she was wealthy, had the already mentioned brown hair, and beautiful blue eyes, a North-German accent, light understanding, a charming speech and an insatiable sexual appetite. She was the only daughter of her widowed mother Edeltraud and they had several apartment houses in Hamburg. At that moment she was ahead of me as undergraduate or degree candidate, preparing her diploma thesis or degree dissertation about the US federal reserve system. I still had to obtain 2 certificates of participation in 2 advanced seminars before becoming a degree candidate. My apartment was that semester the best place for her to work on her thesis and as well as for the following semester to prepare the final exams for the degree. After taking her diploma, she stayed one more semester in Heidelberg, looking for a job. She finally landed a good one in Hamburg and we appointed to meet in there after I had successfully finished my degree dissertation about money bank management and had absolved final exams for the diploma.

After finishing my studies in summer semester 79, I visited her for 2 weeks in Hamburg. As it was my first time in the city, she took some days off to show me the town.

Their house was located in Liebermann Street and looked from the outside very Hanseatic with a great touch of understatement. Unlike the exterior the interior was overwhelming: the furniture was made of Honduran rosewood and Irish leather. As I was told later, Monika's father, Wilhelm, was paid for one big business during the post-war period by one business partner with some cubic meters of Honduran rosewood, whose scientific name is Dalbergia stevensonii, and that Wilhelm partially sold to another business partner, a carpenter with a small factory in Wedel, a town close to Hamburg, and arranged with him the manufacture of the furniture with the wood Wilhelm still had. At first glance, I was unable to correctly classify the wood, because unlike other rosewood kinds it had an untypical red-rosy color, but its sound test was correct: I gentle knocked on it and got the typical crisp sound without noise. The lithographies on the walls and the Rosenthal porcelain also had similar backgrounds.

The introduction to her mother was Hanseatic polite unlike the warm welcome embrace Monika gave me while her mother swallowed hard and tried to look indifferent.

- "Leave your suitcase here, we three go right now for a walk in town" Monika said with a provoking look to her mother who still tried to look indifferent while taking her purse

- "I'll be delighted to do so because the trip with the train was long enough for me" I said and let my bag fall down on the spot.

For that first tour, we had to walk to Bahrenfeld in order to take the S1 of the rapid mass transit railway network to Jungfernstieg and Edeltraud explained me the history of the rapid transit while carefully watching her steps on the cobblestone pavement:

- "Mr. Pages, do you know that our rapid transit was already inaugurated on 16 July1866 as Verbindungsbahn Klosterthor-Altona?"

- "No Mrs. Lachmann, I had no idea of this" I said trying to keep balance during my walking

- "Well, on 5 December 1906 the Hamburg-Altona Stadt- und Vorortbahn started with stream trains the route we are now using, that is to say Hamburg-Altona-Wedel and vice versa" she said leading me to the left to cross the street at the pedestrian way to reach the S1 station

- "Is that right? That is very interesting, indeed!" I said waiting for the green light at the pedestrian way

- "The line was electrified in 1907" Monika added at the time we started crossing the street.

At the station we didn't have to wait long for the S1 which we took to Jungfernstieg.

At Jungfernstieg we walked around Rathaus, Arkaden and Alster. The first thing one learns about Hamburg is the Alster, an affluent of the Elbe River, joining the Elbe in central Hamburg. Unlike the Elbe, the Alster is a non-tidal and slow-flowing river with two artificial lakes, if we omit mentioning the Small Alster. The two artificial lakes were created in central Hamburg many centuries ago, namely known as Inner Alster, and Outer Alster, a precious recreational area, that means: both lakes, and the place where most Hamburgers go sailing. Famous inhabitants of the Alster are the white swans. We walked around the Inner Alster and had lunch at Vier Jahreszeiten.

After lunch we walked around Neuer Wall, Alsterfleet and arrived to Michel. Michel is the knick name of the church St Michaelis, another landmark of Hamburg with its sculpture above the main entrance representing St Michael's victory over the devil. The last reconstruction from 1786 was the church existing at my time. Then, we walked down along Ditm.-Koel Street to the Landungsbrücken, most known in English as St Pauli Piers, Landing Stages or Landing Bridges.

Edeltraud continued the guided tour:
- "The Port of Hamburg, landing stages and warehousing with transhipment facilities are the country's Gateway to the World, and the port is one of the busiest ports in Europe. The Speicherstadt or warehouse district is a large wharf area on the northern shore of the Elbe and is integral part of the free port" she said guiding us to the next pedestrian light
- "A very big area and not easy to walk" I dared say looking at the tricky cobblestone pavement we just had left behind us after the large walk
- "Indeed, we are now tired and will take the bus back home. On the way between downtown and Altona, we show you from the bus Sankt Pauli, the red-light district of Hamburg and the street Reeperbahn, meaning ropewalk, the most sinful mile, with all kind of restaurants, bars, theaters and nightclubs" Edeltraud said showing us the way to the next bus station
- "On 17 August 1960, the Beatles started their career in "Indra Music Club" at the Große Freiheit" Monika said after taking place at the side of her mother on a double-seat in the bus
- "I know it was the first club in which the Beatles played" I said while I took place at the other side on a single-seat
- "Right, from August 17 until October 3, 1960" Edeltraud said
- "People say the venue was a small, dark and dirty club at the end of the Grosse Freiheit" I noted looking to the street
- " Indeed, this was a difficult decision for the Beatles meaning they had to leave Liverpool to work for an unknown German employer performing for a German speaking audience in an unknown country

with whom the UK had been at war about 15 years before" Monika added in a teaching tone

- "After surviving the torture at Indra, they started on 4 October 1960 playing in the Kaiserkeller, 36 Grosse Freiheit. Indra was closed due to complaints about the noise, I think" Edeltraud finished standing up because we had to leave the bus at our station.

It was a long, nice walking tour, and at home we were happy to sit again, have dinner and go early to bed. Next day the tour was going to be Blankenese. The name means something like 'white promontory in the Elbe River'.

This time we took the bus to Blankenese, a suburban quarter in the borough Altona in the western part of Hamburg and it was already regarded as one of Germany's most affluent neighbourhoods.

- "Mr. Pages you tell us please when you feel tired of walking" Edeltraud said in a frankly tone

- "It is going to be a heavy duty tour, because the hillside residences boast many tiny streets and some 4,864 stairs and no lift" Monika added with a smart glance on her eyes.

We had lunch at 12 and decided to go down to the river and walk back via Falkensteiner Ufer, Strandweg, Elbuferweg, Teufelsbrücke, Hindenburgpark, Schröders Elbpark and Himmelsleiter. The walk along the river was easy, even and we all enjoyed it very much and kept talking:

- "Hamburg is indeed, a city state with remarkable corners" I said happy to walk on even pavement

- "Well, not only remarkable corners but with also remarkable people..." Edeltraud said removing some sand from her left shoe

- "...like Uwe Seeler" Monika exhibited her knowledge

- "I know the national soccer player from Hamburger SV" I said feeling smart scoring a point

- "Udo Lindenberg..." Edeltraud added in dreamy mood

- "The rock musician living at Atlantic Hotel with a peculiar feel for the German language" I said not knowing if I was right

- "...and don't forget Helmut Schmidt" Monika exhibited again her knowledge

- "...The actual Chancellor of our Federal Republic..." Edeltraud said with a proud tone in her voice

- "...and his effective management during the 1962 flood in Hamburg..." I added happy to be able to contribute with something to the talk

- "...on 17 February 1962 with approximately 315 deaths" Edeltraud stressed with the same proud tone in her voice

- "He ignored the German constitution and overstepped his legal authority using the army for internal affairs" I said as we arrived to their place.

This was my first warm conversation with Edeltraud. Characteristic for the people in Hamburg is to be polite but reserved. Edeltraud was not an exception and it took me long to get as close as necessary to her. At the time we were introduced, I called her Mrs. Lachmann, and she called me Mr. Pages; only after the first week she offered me to call her Edeltraud, that means: she offered to call me Richard in exchange, but still not using "du" to address each other. That came just later.

At the river side of the Elbe there were many walking ways, and after the good experience we frequently walked, sometimes with Edeltraud. It was our first approach, but the best one was to play German "skat", a three player trick taking card game, with both cats, and to let Edeltraud explain me all about skat in a private crash course before we started playing together:

- "Mr. Pages, do you know that the word "Skat" itself is derived from the Italian word "scarto, scartare", in the meaning of to discard or reject. Its relative "scatola" means a box or a place for safe-keeping" she explained this in a teacher's manner

- "No I didn't know that, Mrs. Lachmann" I said and thought, it was a very emotional game for my cats and knew they loved cheating and I would let them do so

- "Let's talk about your practical experience in skat. Have you ever played it before?" Edeltraud asked. With an inquisitive look

- "Not really, sometimes I had watched people playing and just have a light idea of the game: I know the main attraction of this game is that of the bidding process. After the cards have been dealt, and before the deal is played out, a bidding or auction, in German: Reizen, is held to decide who is going to be the declarer for the round, that is to say the winner of the Reizen becomes declarer, and the minimum game value the declarer needs to win, depending on the type of play the declarer declares to be played" I said proud of my knowledge

- "Do you know how many people can play in a round?" Edeltraud asked again to make sure I understood the game

- "Skat is a game for three players but can also be played by four players sitting out the dealer the round that was dealt" I responded like best pupils use to do

- "That's a good base to start. At the beginning of each round, one player becomes "declarer" and the other two players become the "defending team". The two defenders are not allowed to communicate in any way except by their choice of cards to play" she said this thinking of the contrary, well, I could feel both cats had a long experience cheating in this context

- "We play according to the official rules, Mr. Pages, if you don't mind" Edeltraud said in a businesslike tone

- "That's alright for me" I said accepting my fate and Monika added:

- "We can play the three coexisting varieties as they emerge"

- "I know", I said feeling smart; "you mean Suit, Grand and Null".

- "That is correct, Mr. Pages!" Edeltraud added having doubts whether I knew the meaning of what I was saying

- "Do you know the difference?" Monika explicitly asked

- "As far as I remember, the varieties differ in suit order, scoring and even overall goal to achieve" I said in a convincing tone

- "As Mum already said, each round of the game starts with a bidding phase to set the declarer and the required minimum game value", Monika said one more time

- "I know" I said again in a polite tone

- "Well, you probably don't know that ten tricks are played, players take trick points and each card has a face value..." Monika said thinking she got me

- "I didn't know that, indeed" I said thinking she got me

- "But not in Null games..." Edeltraud added in her best teacher's tone

- "And each card is worth that number of points for the player winning the trick", Monika said in a different teacher's tone

- "Right and the total face value of all cards is 120 points. Declarer must take at least 61 points in tricks in order to win that round of the game. Otherwise, the defending team wins the round" Edeltraud continued her lecture

- "I hope I can keep the many rules in mind" I said feeling poorly

- "I am sure you will after having some practical experiences with us" Monika said not accepting contradiction

- "Points from tricks are not directly added to the players' overall score; they are used only to set the outcome of the game, which means win or loss for declarer" Edeltraud continued the class

- "But don't forget, although winning by certain margins may increase the score for that round" Monika specified with a malicious smile

- "After each round, a score is awarded in accordance with the game value. If declarer wins he obtains a positive score, if he loses the score is doubled and subtracted from declarer's tally" Edeltraud said looking to me with inquiring eyes

- "Further details will be discussed as they arise during training, so you can take your time to understand the game, we won't rush you" Monika added in a benevolent tone

- "Well, Mr. Pages, these are more or less the most important rules you should know about skat before starting training with us" Edeltraud finished the lecture.

That evening my training started and we played until late in the night until we all went satisfied to bed; Monika and Edeltraud because they finally had a third man for skat, in spite of being a trainee willing to learn and play with them, and I because I had found an access to the family.

The second time I came to Hamburg Monika suggested that I gave up my apartment in Heidelberg and move to her house in Hamburg. Edeltraud also agreed on the deal. This was perfect for my plans.

Before marrying her I checked that her mother was also diabetic, and consequentially I decided to marry Monika and clear both cats

I tried to keep track of the group and kept in touch with the ladies, but did not consider necessary to tell them I married Monika on 17 November 1979, a Saturday.

Monika and Edeltraud had a house between Altona and Blankenese in Liebermann Street and 2 apartment houses in Schiller Street, and one more in Behn Street, all three in Altona. It was an ownership community founded many years ago by her father Wilhelm. In this case, I wasn't going to suggest any change as long as Edeltraud lived. The first step was to find an adequate opportunity with a good alibi to clear mother cat. My chance came as Monika had a seminar in Saint Peter Ording in June 1980. We decided that I would join her there and we were going to prolong the stay for two more nights. I scheduled to arrive on 19 June, Thursday night, so I could give mother cat a shot and make sure to have an alibi. I decided to give her the shot that Thursday night before departure, changing syringes before leaving and making sure the shot had worked. Edeltraud was going to be alone at home during the whole night letting the shot come into effect. She was found next morning dead in her bed by the cleaning woman. It was the usual routine: The cleaning woman called us at the hotel; and gave us the news; I called the doctor and the funeral home from the other phone, and we told the cleaning woman to wait until we returned.

The doctor had arrived and examined Edeltraud's body, decided the cause of death was heart failure and signed the death certificate by the time we came. Then the body was transported and prepared immediately for cremation.

The funeral home took care of all formalities like publishing the obituary in the newspapers as well as sending out the invitations to relatives, friends, and employees to attend the funeral ceremony at the local church. After the burial, mourners were invited to an Inn along the Elbe for a buffet meal. Plenty of wine, coffee and drinks were served. It was the German after-funeral feast "Leichenschmaus".

Weeks later, after clearing all formalities with the authorities, Monika was upset due to the high tax she had to pay emerging from inheritance. The only plus point in this matter were the 2 life insurances with a coverage amount of 250,000 Deutsch Mark each, both had closed years ago after Wilhelm's death. Life insurance death benefits were also tax-free in Germany at that time. I managed to convince Monika to create an offshore brass plate company to doctor our balances. The new company allowed, of course; to each of us to having all rights and full access to all accounts of the company, also to my old accounts. A risky construction in case I would not have my emergency exit thanks to the trick I had up my sleeve.

We had to clear with the banks, lawyers and tax consultant the legal and tax points emerging for this purpose. In this matter, there were so many points to observe during the proceedings. We then sold Monika's properties to our offshore brass plate company at the lowest credible price to screw down tax. We also gave us ourselves a special manager contract to protect our health and retirement package. In this case, we didn't have to consider the Scottish inheritance law between spouses. I thought it was better to let sleeping dogs lie.

We also agreed on naming the other partner beneficiary of our life insurances, just to avoid problems, as I said.

Then, we were glad to be back to normal life, well, I was glad to be back to normal life with no more skat to play... Monika was no more upside down, and I just had to satisfy her insatiable sexual appetite the time I was in Hamburg...

Our relationship degenerated into a pure sexual relationship. The only breaks I had were my stays in Edinburgh. I knew I couldn't keep pace with her for long, maybe just a few months. I had to find a solution, a kind of peace of mind, I had no choice. So I planned to clear the cat before August 1981 and make sure to have an alibi. I decided to give her the shot the night I departed to Edinburgh on 14

July 1981, a Tuesday, for a regular meeting at the factory, changing syringes before leaving and making sure the shot had worked. She was going to be alone at home during the whole night letting the shot come completely into effect and would be found next morning by the cleaning woman.

As expected, following morning, the cleaning woman called me at the meeting in the factory and gave me the bad news. I told her to proceed as last time, call the doctor and wait until I came back. I gave the news to the funeral home and told them the doctor was on his way; they should wait for the doctor at my house. For my part, I would be taking the next flight to Hamburg. The doctor arrived, examined Monika's body and decided the cause of death was heart failure and signed the death certificate. Then the body was transported and prepared for cremation. No more body, no more evidences.

After the burial, I proceeded as last time; I cleared all legal matters with the banks, lawyers and tax consultant, let them do all necessary name rearrangements in the construction and hoped to overcome from the nasty cold I had got at the cemetery. Time was running fast. The postponed meeting was set for 28 July 1981 and I took the plane to Edinburgh on 27 July. I wanted to come back to my real life with standard meetings at the factory... I wanted my healthy life back, but people around had very nasty colds too and the meeting at the factory turned out to be a concert of coughs this time.

Afterwards I had a long walk on the Leith beach, thinking about the deleterious effects of the numerous storms of this life of mine... It was quite chilly but I was dressed in a bear way... I concluded I needed indeed a "changement d'air"... and I reached my place in a cheerful mood.

Chapter 4

Fatema Dochta Zakariya

Lena, the cook from the agency, had dinner almost ready as I arrived home at 19:20h and I ate enough trying with pleasure to feed the nasty cold. After dinner, I checked the correspondence at my desk still in the same cheerful mood on this 28 July 1981 as the phone rang bringing me back to reality:
- "Hi Richard, here is Fatema!"
- "Hi Fatema, it is so nice to hear your voice! What's up, doc?" this was an allusion to Bug's Bunny I always used because she loved to read such magazines.
- "It was not easy to find you at home. Just wanted to keep you posted: I definitely moved last month from Kabul to London and wonder if you want to drop in for a visit any time you want" Fatema said expecting a positive answer
- "I just arrived to Edinburgh yesterday, that's why. I would be delighted to do so, let me check my agenda and I give you a call back" I said and she gave me her number in London.

Fatema was a nice girl with parents from Afghanistan, same studies and member of the group. Her name was Fatema Dochta Zakariya, Dochta meaning "daughter of" deriving from some Indo-Germanic root close to German "Tochter des". Well, at that moment I just thought of her black hair and dark eyes. Due to the fact that this time we spoke English on the phone I missed her beautiful accent in German, but with the attractive and sunny nature reflected in her voice she managed to increase my cheerful mood.

I checked my agenda, called her back and we decided to meet two weeks later in August 1981 in London. She gave me her address:
- "I live just a few blocks away from Victoria Station at Cambridge Street close to St Gabriel's Church" she said in a sweet tone
- "I hope it is easy to find" I responded in a businesslike manner
- "Just take Wilton Road down to Warwick Way until Cambridge Street, turn to the right and look for the church. That's it!" she

declaimed in a triumphal way... No, I think she said this in a very convincing but not persuading way. This was the way she was. I was going to stay a week at her place and she wanted to plan some tours for me as this was my first time in London, excluding the airport.

Two weeks later, I arrived easy, as she said, to her place short before tea-time. The way by car was more than 400 miles and therefore I preferred to take the plane this time and thus arrived not stressed, it was not hectic at Heathrow Airport or in Victoria Station. Fatema lived in a huge apartment her grandparents had bought decades ago with butler James and cook-lady Jenny. At the time I came, James grandson was then the third in office, number four was already "in process" finishing his apprenticeship, and Jenny's granddaughter Mary was in charge of the kitchen. Afghan tradition I thought.

The apartment was fitted up with Chippendale style furniture in cherry with elaborated pieces made for wealthy people of the 19th century: cabriole legs, broken arch pediments and artistic carvings blended with simple lines breathing a timeless air.

After unpacking my suitcase in my room we had tea and discussed the planned tours for the next days sitting very comfortable on vintage buttoned green leather arm chairs:

- "Before dinner we go for a short walk around the block, if you don't mind, Richard" she said looking into her empty Koenigliche Porzellan Manufaktur cup with exquisitely balanced Rocaille proportions, a perfect fusion of form and function, as a noiseless James came into the room, took the corresponding KPM porcelain teapot and refilled her cup, turned to me and did the same with my empty KPM cup and left the room the same way he had come in

- "Not at all, that would be perfect for me" I said reading the seal with the number 925 on the tea spoon and admiring James timing and the way Fatema communicated without words with him

- "Tomorrow we walk the area between Buckingham Palace and Trafalgar Square, that means: Palace, Queen Victoria Memorial, St James's Park, The Mall, Trafalgar Square, Pall Mall, Piccadilly, Green Park, and Horse Guard Parade" she suggested with clear voice reaching me the scones

- "I would be delighted to walk that area, but I am not sure if it is not too much for you" I answered knowing she wouldn't reduce the length of the tour while putting some clotted cream on my half-scone

- "There is no excuse for lazy boys!" was her clear war declaration taking the bit between her teeth and biting into her half-scone

- "Alright, alright, we proceed as suggested" I said giving up and looking for the strawberry jam as I preferred to put jam on top of the clotted cream

- "The second tour could be the tower of London, Tower Bridge and St Paul's Cathedral..." she said expecting no contradiction and having a sip of tea

- "That would be perfect!" I said gentle as a lamb and having also a sip of that delicious Darjeeling second flush

- The third tour would be Tate Galleries, Westminster Abbey, the Themes, House of Parliament, Big Ben, Westminster Bridge, Waterloo Bridge" she continued in the same way

- "Considering the English cuisine, I would suggest, we take lunch from home and make a break at some adequate places as we want" I said trying to give the impression of maturity and that Mary could consider this a compliment as I knew James was hidden somewhere listening and would pass it on

- "That is a very good idea, Richard. James, please tell Mary to do so!" she said addressing James, who in fact suddenly appeared in the room

- "Yes, madam!" James said and disappeared noiseless from the room.

After tea, we did the short walk hand in hand around the blocks and had a very good dinner Mary had prepared for us. Later we heard some music and went early to bed.

Tour 1 was very nice and we did a lot of walk, hand in hand again, without getting excessively tired. The area between Buckingham Palace and Trafalgar Square was crowded with people as usual, of course, but we enjoyed every second of the tour.

Tour 2 was a very thirsty one on a golden day. Tower of London was fatiguing, Tower Bridge was a nice walk but too much traffic, and St Paul's Cathedral was a nice place to sit and recover a little. We were happy to get back to her place and to stretch out the legs for a while.

Tour 3 was pregnant with culture and arts in the Tate Galleries and a large and nice walking, hand in hand again, around Westminster, the river, and parliament, Big Ben, Westminster Bridge and Waterloo Bridge. After the experience of the day before, we did a lot of breaks in-between and drank a lot of water, so that we came back to her place with our feet in a better mood.

Day four of my stay was a sunny Sunday, so we had to go to Hyde Park to listen to the speakers around there.

Day five of my stay was reserved for a good time visiting in the evening the "Mousetrap" play at Saint Martins Theatre in the West Street, Agatha Christie at her best.

On day six we did some shopping before having a wonderful dinner at her place and made plans for the next meeting:

- "We can meet next time in Edinburgh if you want, doc" I said hopping she would agree

- "Oh yes, I would be delighted because I didn't see much of Edinburgh at your wedding" she said with a poker face

- "Yes, I remember, the group was just talking and talking in the backyard. In this case, I'll be your guide and you can stay as long as you want at my place" I said thinking to avoid conflicts

- "Let's say one week?" she said with an innocent asking glance on her eyes

- "One week as you desire, do you think 20-27 November is alright, doc?" I asked checking my agenda

- "I think so" she said after checking hers

- "You tell me the flight number and arriving time so that I may fetch you at the airport" I said in a pleased tone

- "Take it for granted" she answered in the same tone.

After dinner, we went to the movies to watch Bug's Bunny and enjoyed the peaceful walk back to her place. I had the impression time was running too fast when we were together. Our parenthesis was of outer space and enchanting.

She immediately booked her fare to Edinburgh and called to keep me posted once she got her ticket. She called again 3 days before departure, to give me the itinerary so that I could fetch her at the airport. After she unpacked her suitcase I showed her the changes in house before having tea and then we walked a little through the parks. We came back and prepared dinner together and enjoyed the long lasting meal. That night brought me back to a man's life breathing normally. It was delicious not to switch off during that week and to keep talking with her like the first night:

- "I am very angry" I said in a serious tone

- "Against me or against you?" she asked not knowing how to react

- "Against myself, of course, because sometimes I don't find my hidden ways in Edinburgh I want to share with you" I replied very upset

- "It really doesn't matter and I hope it doesn't hurt" she stressed in a Bug's Bunny manner

- "Of course it hurts because it always happens when we are together. It is as if a part of my mind is being obliterated and prevents me from being fully aware when you are around" I said mulish
- "It is the same with me, and you know I hate the feeling of losing control, especially knowing you are close to me" she said on heat
- "I think we feel the same, as if something is broken and cannot be mended" I philosophized not knowing if I was right
- "Right, I think it is just because we are attempting to find everyday something the other might like to get, and that is not necessary" she said just like that in her uncomplicated way
- "It is just that I feel frustrated due to my failed tries" I complained looking for comfort
- "What shall I say? It affects the way we think of each other and how we get along with the other" she said trying to console me, what she in fact did
- "I cannot stand it" I categorically added feeling her hand clinging to my left arm
- "Take it easy, I know what you give, what you enable that I overcome" she tried to explain
- "You deserve more than being a sex friend. That is not what you have been looking for" I stated not knowing me anymore
- "Your situation is probably similar to the one you already lived once and feel now uncomfortable, but this doesn't matter as long as you don't compare both situations. You know I like hanging around in nowhere with my hand in yours or should I say with your hand in mine feeling the world around" she said the way women can point out matters
- "I only want good and not a wounding relationship with you…" and she stopped my speech pressing her lips to mine.

After that delicious week, I came back to normal life with a lot of correspondence to check and administrative work to do and a lot of warm thoughts which still remained very warm. Fatema was in the same mood as she told me at our following meeting in London and in that mood I dared speak with her about my deepest secrets:
- "Fatema, I would like to tell you two things concerning my life and my parents and that I kept very deep in my inside until now"
- "You mean you never mentioned it to anyone?"
- "Yes, I never spoke of it before to any person, well, concerning my life, and concerning my parents excluding the authorities and doctors, I want you to be the first one to share this matter with" I said very seriously
- "Please go ahead" she said full of expectation

- "I give you a brief overview with no further details: I killed some people. As I said now I give you no more details to protect you" I said expecting her reaction

- "That's alright for me because I know you will give me further details when you consider it is safe for me. However I must confess that I also killed some people..."

- "Really..." I said perplex

- "It happened in Afghanistan during my last stay in there at a land tour: we were ambushed by bandits, but fortunately we were able to fire back, contact the second vehicle behind us and acting together we could make retaliatory moves against the assailants, finally overran the ambush positions and killed all attackers"

- "That comes as a shock for me, why didn't you say a word before? You know I am with you!"

- "I was confident that you were the right person and was waiting for the right moment... But what is the matter about your parents?" she asked before I disappeared in the kitchen

-."You know I never talk about my parents" I said shamefaced reappearing in the living room with two mugs in one hand and a bottle of sparkling water in the other

- "Yes I know that" she said feeling it was not an easy task for me to talk about this matter

- "Thank you for never asking; the reason is that my parents abused of me at the time I was a child" I said trying to keep my head while filling water in the mugs

- "Do you mean, they mistreated you physically, sexually or psychologically, your own caregivers?" she said losing her temper and snatching at one mug

- "Yes, the first level was sexual abuse by both with additional physical and psychological mistreatments when I didn't immediately do what they wanted" I said trying not to lose my voice and having a sip of water

- "Oh no, how could it be possible?" she said bursting into violent sobs and wolfing down a water gulp

- "My mother was a high qualified official in the counter-espionage of the Army and my father was her slave" I said in an angry voice looking embarrassed into my mug

- "That is not a reason for abusing you; their own child!" she said very upset and taking it to heart

- "My mother having sex with me and my father watching us, both having great sexual stimulation" I specified softly having one more sip of water in the vain effort to avoid crying

- "What degeneration and what a humiliation for you... and all that deliberated harming you" she said in a very angry tone moving like a tiger in a cage

- "It lasted a few years until the authorities came behind their doing and removed me from my family" I said after recovering a little

- "And what happened next?" she asked softly taking me under her wing

- "I had to go to a children's home in Bremen" I disclosed feeling better

- "Wait, why Bremen? I thought you come from Michelstadt" she asked astonished

- "Yes and no; the whole story is that I was born in Bremen, and first grew up in that city with my parents until the authorities intervened, took me into custody, then found a better place for me in a different location, faraway from my parents because they were always trying to trace me through any legal or half legal channel" I said businesslike

- "I see they couldn't let you in peace" she said still angry and having one more water gulp

- "Well, Bremen was not the best spot to keep me away from my parents, who knew the city very well and had a lot of contacts" I added in a black hat tone

- "I would say they developed the typical criminal energy people do in such cases" she said in a prostrated mood and showing me her protective soul

- "Right, and that's how I came to Michelstadt in a special children's home, finished high school with good records, received financial help from the Hesse State for my further education and got the admission to the university of Heidelberg where we met" I said feeling safe under her protection

- "Your first ray of hope..." she said in a sweet mood

- "Well, the harm they did to me left deep footprints in my inside, but somehow I managed to appear as a normal being, I hope" I said in a confession tone

- "Indeed, I can only speak for me and I had a very good impression of you, you know that" she said that embracing me

- "Yes I know that and that's why we are now talking about this matter" I said returning her embrace in a soft way

- "The problems with your parents are incredible, especially because they didn't care at all about potential harm to your health, survival, development, integrity or even dignity..." she said with great indignation

- "Doctors told me later that my parents did not understand the severity of the problem. My protection was never a goal for them. It was not a matter of how to raise a child, but a vital matter of escaping from the professional life they couldn't overcome" I said pretending to be cool

- "I think the effects of child sexual abuse on you as a victim cannot be really estimated..." it was a profound eye-to-eye silent and high-tension watching before I dared interrupt the tension and asked her with trembling voice:

- "Do you want to marry me?"

- "Yes, yes, yes, yes I want it very much... you know I love your question..." she answered in deep ecstasy

- "I don't know much about words..." I said in a modest tone

- "Nice words... Warm thoughts..." she dared to contradict

- "I thank you tenderly" was the last thing I remember of that night.

So it came by itself that we decided that day to move together to Edinburgh:

- "Fatema, we have the option to stay in London or in Edinburgh, what you would prefer?" I asked

- "Considering all factors, I think Edinburgh would the best choice due to the garden" she said thinking of the future

- "Garden is good for children. If we select Edinburgh, we have some modifications to do in the house to accommodate properly James and Mary" I said knowing she would completely agree with me on this point

- "You are right, we need some additional and comfortable rooms for James and Mary" she said pleased that I already considered taking Mary and James with us to Edinburgh

- "I think we can set up on the garage some additional and comfortable rooms for them, let me check this with the architect" I concluded.

Next morning, I asked the architect to make some suggestions for the following Friday:

- "The best option for your house is using precast elements with a roof connection to the house on top of the already for such purpose prepared garage" he said very pleased of my enquiry

- "If you confirm that this is the easiest and fastest way for the set up, you are welcome to make the necessary estimation" I said

- "At the time we built the garage, Sean Downing, your former father in law, ordered to build the garage prepared for such an extension" he explained with a twinkle in his eye

- "That means the previous work is already done?" I asked pleased to hear that

- "Indeed, we can immediately start with it. There are two main factors in favour of precasting: formwork and concrete. The importance of well made and accurate formwork is essential for a good construction and the good mix design and careful placing to avoid air bubbles and good consolidation are the keys to successful precast elements" he explained as master of his profession

I called Fatema, gave her a briefing and we decided to use on the garage prefabricated or, as the architect said, precast elements with a roof connection to the house due to the reasons the architect had explained.

We informed Mary and James about our plans and as they had no objections, we scheduled to move to Edinburgh once the construction was finished in January 1982.

December 1981 we spent together in London preparing our marriage in March 1982. Fatema explained me all about Afghan weddings amid Pashtun people: the special song sung at the beginning, "Ahesta Boro" meaning "walk slowly", the Nikah or Islamic marriage ceremony, the Henna or originally the little incisions cut into the bride and groom's palm and at the present substituted by the plant henna, also spelled hennah, which the mother of the groom put onto the bride's palm, cover it with a fine and shiny cloth, and the bride's mother put the henna on the pinkie finger of the groom and cover it with the cloth. Then the meal follows with different kinds of rice, kabobs, Afghan bread... After dessert, they cut the cake while people sing traditional songs like "Baada Baada Elahee Mubarak Baada", meaning "congratulations, I gave you my heart now I leave it to God"... Afterwards Attan, the national dance, happens. At that moment my head reeled and I was glad that Fatema's family was Christian and stressed it:

- "I am really glad that you are Christian..." I said with great relief

- "I know what you mean. You don't have to worry about strange wedding ceremonies and other religions" she said it teasing me

- "Well, I am not sure I wouldn't do it for you" I answered in a similar teasing tone

- "It is easy for you to say that, knowing my family immigrated to Great Britain already in 1892 and that they were Christian long before" she said without excitement over my wording

- "Of course, we are going to be married by the registrar, an easy task for me" I said in a modest tone.

However, family links were very strong for her and she gave me a briefing concerning the whole closest relatives from her side:
- "Just for the file, my father died in 1978 and my mother in 1980" she started her lecture
- "Yes, you told me that already and also that the other closest relatives are still alive" I admitted
- "Indeed, my father had 2 brothers: Sami and Nika" she continued the briefing
- "Still alive" I insisted
- "Shut up! Sami is married to Zhora, born Stori, and they have two sons: Nuri and Arman" she continued looking to me like teachers use to do when pupils don't behave the way they should
- "You said one is single…" I remarked in an innocent tone
- "Good boy! Nuri is single at the present time. Arman is married to Nesrin, born Ehsandmand, and they have one daughter: Kira, single at the present" Fatema continued pleased
- "I got it" I said also pleased
- "Nika, the second brother of my father, is married to Lina, born Fani, and they have one son and one daughter: Anil and Ava" she continued still pleased
- "Go ahead" I insisted while stroking her back with my hands
- "Keep your hands under control and listen! Anil is married to Samira, born Rahimi, and they have three sons: Mehmet, Samir and Idris, all still single at the present" she said again teacherlike
- "Please continue" I dared say in best-pupil manner
- "Ava is married to Farid Nazemi, and they have two sons, Amar and Navid, both single at the present" she stopped looking to me
- "I suppose here ends the family chronicle of your father" I said and tried to look smart
- "Smart boy… my mother have one brother: Arian Tarzi" she said very pleased
- "Go ahead" I requested her to continue with a delighted smile on my lips
- "Arian is married to Xezal, born Ghubar, and they have 3 sons: Milad, Tarik and Haris, all single at the present" she finished trying to hide her stimulated mood
- "Now I have them all together. We continue tomorrow if you don't mind" I said while stroking her body
- "I think I am not able to stop your hands stroking my mug…" she said with pleased resignation before we started making paradise love.

After long considerations and reconsiderations, we decided the following days to invite her closest relatives, which meant, the brothers of her father and of her mother with all their children. We contacted them and kept them posted at that early stage about our plans and they all wanted to come to our wedding in March 1982.

Concerning finances, Fatema's parents had a similar construction to the one I had for finances. So we just had to draw up the plenary powers at the notary and to register them later at the corresponding banks and companies, no big task at all compared with the selection of the wedding guests.

We married as scheduled on 18 March 1982, a sunny Thursday, in Edinburgh, and we celebrated with her closest relatives, 6 legal representatives and a delegation of the factory. Mary and James supervised the ceremonies, leased attendants and catering services. The group was not invited.

Everything worked perfectly and afterwards we gave Mary and James the following week off while we were recovering in Hamburg.

After checking insurances, Fatema had one, I had one and Mary and James III and IV had each of them a risk insurance, we decided we were all set in this matter.

Back to normal healthy life we enjoyed the very busy time in our retired citizens' life until the factory take-over in November 1982. The transaction was made as desired and I managed to avoid paying too much tax due to my financial model. One can call it tax allowance...

Once again we spent Christmas at home and later travelled a little through Europe and Asia checking the different accounts and companies we had. In this context we avoided to visit Afghanistan due to the well-known reasons and decided to delete the country from our travelling list due to the political and economic development in the country.

In January 1984, Fatema consulted the doctor because she was not feeling well, she complained of having a metallic taste in her mouth, morning sickness, and an increase in weight... and then she got the news from her doctor: she was pregnant and we both were very happy. We were full of expectation regarding this new chapter in our lives.

We decided to reduce golf and avoid toxic substances like caffeine, alcohol and other unhealthy habits, but she also started having regular check ups, etc., to avoid getting unpleasant diseases and reduce the risk of miscarriages. She was getting used to her new body and we were preparing for the new baby on the way.

One morning it was business as usual. I sat down at my desk with a cup of hot tea when I heard Fatema crying in her office; I rushed to her side:
- "What is wrong with you? Are you alright?" I asked
- "No, I am not alright, not at all, I just feel awful... My soul had crashed" she said
- "Try not to panic. You know these moods are manifestations deriving from the pregnancy. They feel real although they are not real, but we must take them always seriously because they may hurt your soul" I said trying to calm her
- "You make me feel good! Please stay with me for a while. I want to feel the warmness of your body, to feel melted with you" she supplicated for what I already was giving her
- "You know you can come to me any time you feel like that. You are not alone, I am with you, and we overcome the crisis together if you let me help you" I said imploring her
- "I know you are always with me and it helps a lot. What a stupid mood!" she said shamefaced
- "Well, you must be conscious of it and control the temptation to panic. Not always an easy task for smart girls like you" I said teacherlike with a light waggish under tone
- "Stop kidding and embrace me, warm body and warm thoughts" she said with an angelical smile
- "Your wish is my command, warm body and warm thoughts" I said with a demoniacal smile feeling her melting in my arms.

Afterwards we had a very fulfilling time. It was the right approach for both of us and everything was soon back to normal. We overcame with such common and intensive moments all subsequent bad moods she had and we developed strong links between us, more than ever. We both were possessed of each other in a holy way.

We thought a lot about the future and what it was going to look like, and we spent a ridiculous amount of time preparing for possible scenarios. It was the way we were wired.

We had everything physically ready for our child's arrival, and we thought that we were pretty mentally prepared for it, too.

On April 1984 she decided to bring some of her children's furniture she still had in London to Edinburgh by car. Knowing her pigheadedness I suggested that James, the third, should escort her on her 400 miles long way. James the fourth was then already in charge of the London apartment.

After consulting the maps, we selected the route they were going to take: Ebury Bridge, A3214, B319, A4, Heathrow, M25, M4/M23, M40, M42, M6, A74, A702, Buckstone Drive, Braid Road,

Hermitage Drive, Midmar Avenue, Cluny Gardens, Oswald Road, Kilgraston Road, Melville Drive/A700, Hope Park Cres, Buccleuch Street, Meadow Lane. Summa summarum: about 420 miles drive with one overnight stay. I wanted to make sure she wasn't going to overplay her hand this time.

They left London on Tuesday and were supposed to arrive to Edinburgh on Wednesday afternoon. Well, they never arrived, because they were involved in a car accident on the M6, at milestone 391.2. According to police records, a truck with trailer driving in the same direction crashed against the left pier of the bridge and wiped the cars at its right side against the right pier of the same bridge, 6 cars in all, 14 persons were involved in the accident and six of them died. Fatema, our unborn child and James the third were among the victims.

When the accident occurred I was a bit of disconnect. A lot of what happened in the first moment of getting the news threw me for a loop. I was not mentally prepared for digesting the news like I thought I was, and it took me a long time to realize that I was mourning the loss of Fatema and of the child I thought we were going to have.

Our child did not want to be cuddled. It didn't want to feel constricted. Even if it was hurt, it didn't want me to interrupt its memory!

And then something shifted in me. Our child wasn't who we thought it would be; it was who it was supposed to be. My job was to be the best father I could be to it. I felt like one was given what one needed through having a child and I was given the opportunity to learn that one simply cannot plan for everything. Things never come in the package we expect them to come in, and my job as a fictive father was to be able to roll with the punches. If our child is different from what we expected, my job as a parent is to be its biggest advocate and figure out what it was he needed for itself.

I had to identify the bodies, a very painful matter for me. Then the funeral home took care of everything because I was not able to do it by myself. They were indeed very helpful through the process of arranging the funeral. The burial ceremony for both, Fatema and James, took place in the St Margaret's Church close to the Eastern Cemetery of Edinburgh where Fatema was to be buried. James was transported after the ceremony to his original town in Wales to be buried in there.

As a matter of honor, all closest relatives assisted to the funeral. The mass contained: Prayer of St. Francis of Assisi, First Reading Ecclesiastic 18 8-14, Responsorial Psalm David 23, Halleluiah, Gospel St John 12-24, Homily, Apostles' Creed, Oblation,

Sanctus, Anamnesis, Agnus Dei, Lord's Prayer, Communion, Thanksgiving, Family Speeches were done by Sami, Nika and Arian, and I asked Kira to recite the poem On Another's Sorrow by William Blake, then came Incense and Holy Water and finally Procession. The service was accompanied by organ and a soprano, and Laudate Dominum by Mozart, KV339, and Höchster BWV1083 by J. S. Bach, Jauchzet Gott in allen Landen, BWV51 by J. S. Bach were played.

Afterwards we had the usual Leichenschmaus at the Golf Club and then I was left alone with my agony and some of the words by William Blake cutting my heart in pieces: Fatema and our unborn child left, but now alone I don't seek for kind relief. Both of them gave me all their joy, but now alone I don't seek for kind relief. I could always rely on her, but now alone I don't seek for kind relief. I won't sit night and day wiping all my tears away because now alone I don't seek for kind relief... But there is still the magic of their memory in my head... Nice memories... Warm thoughts...

Chapter 5

Frederike Stechow

The whole May was my period of mourning with deep grief for Stella, Fatema and our unborn child. It was the first time I had the opportunity to reconsider the experiences I had with my unique ladies and to strike the balance.

The time with Stella was the delicious time of research and development, exploring new horizons, learning how fulfilling a partnership could be; finally I could evaluate how ephemeral life is, how strong feelings can be here, there or elsewhere when we were together or at our own on these roads that belong to us.

The time with Fatema was the delirious time of intensive communion and tangible spiritual links, the exclusive moments in our everyday lives. It was our necessary quest to investigate through the appearances and beyond the real on the other side of the life mirror where we were, are, and will be only they and me. Yes "they" mean Stella, Fatema and our unborn child, all of us without contradiction, envy, jealousy but with deep love, devotion, and sincerity somewhere in outer space.

End of May I was not afraid to remain myself, to give them what I was, true and present, aware and welcoming, generous and open. Sometimes when they looked at me I believed that they were trying to read in my inside, beyond my glance, under my skin or in my mind. I then knew they were vigilantly smiling and monitoring my actions, recording the words I said, reacting to the gentle warm thought I had...

In June I decided to go out of mourning, to come back to business as usual. I started establishing new premises for creating a different reality for my monetary funds, just in case I would pass away without legal descendants. I didn't want the administration bags all my money. I had to undo the limitations Treasury had invented in this matter. I consulted my lawyers and they suggested creating a legal recognized foundation would be the best way for me. Charitable organizations are non-profit organizations with philanthropic goals.

That was an easy task, but finding an adequate country in and from which the organization was going to operate with best regulations and tax treatment was not that easy. Financial figures, like tax refunds, allowed deductions, etc., were fundamental premises. So we established a charity foundation for abused children in the world registered in Lichtenstein under the name CA84 with operational field at international level. I was not trying to shunt responsibility and pass the buck to someone else, I was able to do it and I was going to do it, period.

We managed to successfully close the project in 16 days and that's why I was glad to receive on 20 June 1984 in the evening a distracting phone call from Aurelia:

- "Hi Richard, here is Aurelia"

- "Hi Aurelia, it is so nice to hear you after such a long time. What can I do for you?"

- "It is just that Anton and I decided, after so many years, to finally marry and I would be pleased if you could be my witness to the wedding"

- "Of course I would be delighted to be your witness. Can you give me the details for the wedding?"

- "I'll send you soon an official invitation, but just for the file: we plan to get married on Monday, 12 November 1984 in Oberjoch, Bad Hindelang, our domicile"

- "I see, you mean: 'hinten lang'..." I said having in mind the whole sentence meaning something like 'back large and front short' with a lot of possible meanings

- "Don't dare say that again!" was her quick response in a hostile tone

- "Why not, it is a magnificent landscape..." I dared say not really believing in what I was saying

- "Of course, my back is a magnificent landscape..." she said with challenging voice

- "I think we better stop here... just tell me who is going to be my counterpart" I asked in my best businesslike tone

- "Anton asked Frederike to be his witness to the wedding and she is willing to do it" she added with a certain suspense note in her voice

- "I first thought that his old pal Henning was going to be his first choice" I said thinking of the propitious opportunity to catch Frederike as my next cat

- "Well, that was his first choice, but after getting the bad news of Henning's fatal climbing accident in the Pyrenees last month..." she stated like a government spokeswoman

- "Oh no, how bad for him and his family" I stated back considering that in the last contact we had for last Christmas Henning said that he was still married but had already filed the petition for divorce from his wife

- "He divorced a few months earlier from his wife, last February, and he was single at the time he died" the spokeswoman continued her communiqué

- "I see we have a lot to talk about at our next meeting" I said trying to find out how the terrain lay

- "Indeed, I suppose you know that Frederike moved recently within walking distance from us in town" she said in a nice enigmatic tone

- "Yes, the last time we talked on the phone she said she was already set in a nice house not far away from yours after leaving Munich where she had a couple of apartment houses she inherited from her parents" I said keeping in my backhand the fact that Frederike had told me she was going to keep her apartment in Munich as a kind of company apartment because from time to time she had to stay in Munich overnight due to works in the houses or household clearances

- "That's right, we are frequently together on the weekends either playing golf or table tennis" she said in a barely audible indiscreet tone

- "You still keep playing table tennis!" I said thinking of the sauna we used to take afterwards in Heidelberg

- "Indeed, we enjoy it very much, but from time to time we also do so some hiking in the near neighbourhood, you know, day tours" she added in a malicious tone I almost didn't get

- "Yes, you are located at a nice spot" I said, considering this valuable information that could give me a good chance to catch my next cat...

- "You don't have to wait until November to meet us, you are welcome any time and I agree with you that we have a lot to talk about" she said in the same malicious tone

- "Is that right?! I'll check my agenda and make suggestions. I think July/August could be a good time" I said certain that I could arrange a meeting any time it could be necessary

- "You won't mind if I inform Frederike about our plan" she said in a higher malicious tone

- "Not at all, feel free to do so! I'll ring you up tomorrow evening to set the meeting time" I answered in a similar malicious tone

- "That would be perfect for me, bye-bye Richard" she said in a soft tone

- "Until tomorrow Aurelia, best regards to Anton" I said trying to sound polite
- "Thank you" she finished with melodious tone.

I immediately checked my agenda and found one possible week in July and another in August. Then I had to prepare my strategy concerning Frederike. As she had already mentioned, she had inherited from her parents a couple of houses, I would say, in best location in Munich, because all houses in Munich downtown have best location, and with the rental receipts she didn't have to work any more, so I thought let's go to work! This time I didn't want to rush but have lot of fun...

I first checked the region where she lived: Bad Hindelang was located at an altitude of 825m and had approx. 5,000 inhabitants; it was a municipality in the district of Oberallgäu. On the other hand, Oberjoch was a sub-municipality of Hindelang, a small village with approx. 200 inhabitants; and was located at 1136m, on the mountain Iseler, its 'backyard' mountain.

The following day we agreed on the phone to meet on calendar week 28 and I had the opportunity to talk to Frederike who coincidentally was at Aurelia's place at the time I called:
- "Glad to hear you again Richard, how are you doing?" Frederike said starting the talk
- "I am fine, thank you, what about you?" I answered in a pleased tone
- "I am fine too. I am looking forward to meeting you on calendar week 28. Please don't forget your hiking shoes" she said in an ambiguous tone
- "I promise I won't forget them, meanwhile behave" I dared say in a demonic tone
- "Knock it off. See you next" she finished.

Obviously, Aurelia and Frederike wanted to meet me. Aurelia was going to marry in short, so I thought she was supposed to be a no-no. Frederike was on the other hand still free and wealthy, so the next time I wanted to make a point of staying at her place.

Time did run fast this time and before realizing it, I already arrived to Iseler Street in Oberjoch on Sunday to meet two thirsty ladies:
- "Welcome to our place Richard" Aurelia said
- "Feel at home Richard" Anton assisted
- "Welcome to Oberjoch Richard, I show you later my place a few meters up the hill on the same street" Frederike said with a dirty smile on her face

- "Thank you for the warm reception, it has been a long time since we were together last time and hope it won't take that long to meet again" I said as Anton took my suitcase and the ladies my two bags after I defended my rucksack from been overtaken by two hungry ladies.
- "We show you your room now and let you powder your nose before meeting in the living room" Aurelia said
- "This is your room, Richard" Anton said
- "Wow, beautiful room, magnificent view and nice photos on the wall; just give me 10 minutes to powder my nose..." I said feeling high pressure in my bladder while smiling
- "The photos are from Frederike" Aurelia said looking nowhere
- "Take your time and let me know if you need any help" Anton said taking the ladies off from my room.

10 minutes later we met again in the living room and I gave each of them a Single Malt Whisky bottle of my favourite medicine which they all highly appreciated. Then we kept talking in the living room, talking in the garden, talking in the kitchen, talking on the way to Frederike's place, talking during the guided tour in her house, talking on the way back to Anton's and Aurelia's place, and talking again in the living room for hours until late in the night. Well, Anton went to bed at 22:00h because he had next day, Monday, early in the morning consults and blood exams to do in his clinic located in Hindelang. As a specialist in internal medicine and working man he had some responsibilities we didn't have.

Next morning I heard when Anton left for the clinic at 06:30h. Before I decided to stand up, the door bell rang and short after that both ladies came in my room with some coffee for me and a malicious glance in their eyes as the owners of passion that can handle any virtue and vice without breaking a sweat, which is another reason why women always win, why women had developed the ability to succeed in doing what they like. Well, they really seduced me and I had to find quickly a solution to the top question, how could I satisfy 2 hungry ladies with my limited resources? I knew two ejaculations were normally possible, two more may occur some times under favourable circumstances, but only super humans could do more, and I was not a superman; that was it for me. So I decided to set our doing in the right order to have a chance to put on simulated ejaculations while giving them the most pleasure I could give: I took a comfortable position lying on my back on the bed and told Frederike to suck my penis while I started sucking Aurelia's clitoris, who was standing upright on her knees on bed with her pussy facing my mouth and watching Frederike sucking it to me. I drove Aurelia crazy with this procedure and she was strongly trembling due to the abdominal contractions she had every time an orgasm happened to her. Meanwhile Frederike enjoyed drinking every drop of my ambrosia continuing softly sucking my best part as asking for more and after a while I told them to change places. I didn't know a place change could be so stimulating for me. The vulvas and clitorises of the ladies were not identical and had a different taste and smell, each of them delicious in their singularity. After I finished in Aurelia's mouth I told her to sit on my penis while I continued kissing Frederike's clitoris. This time I simulated an ejaculation after Aurelia had some orgasms and told them to change places again and after having the ladies a few orgasms I simulated one more ejaculation. We kept doing sex this way during the whole morning until 11:30h and took a shower together before Aurelia left for an hour to prepare lunch for Anton.

That became our morning gymnastic during the whole of my stay in Oberjoch, excepting for the weekend. In the afternoon we had to rush, go shopping and do something for our story to tell. That afternoon we visited Nebelhorn, next day Oberjochsattel, other day Tannheimertal, next Kotbachtal. We did every day a different excursion to one place of interest...

The weekend was reserved for golf and table tennis with Anton. Well, our timetable was adapted to the cleaning woman as they had the same cleaning woman who came Mondays and Thursdays to Frederike's house and Tuesdays and Fridays to Aurelia's house, that meant on Tuesday and Friday we had to move very early to Frederike's place. This was a funny situation for me but not for the ladies; obviously they loved to play with fire and to have sex together with me while Anton was working.

After that experience we knew we were going to have the same procedure every time we would be together. My problem was that Aurelia wasn't diabetic and I had to find a way to escape after I cleared my cat. Next time was August. I invited the ladies to spend a week with me in Hamburg and we had a good time together with no day-off for me. In September we were one week together at Frederike's place in Oberjoch and visited Jungholz, Aggenstein and Grünten. In October we had the same procedure in Hamburg, again with no day-off for me. November was wedding and our meeting didn't come off. We just celebrated Anton's and Aurelia's wedding in a traditional way and Anton was not suspicious at all of our doing. On the contrary, he was happy we were together and told me how he managed to get the clinic in Hindelang:

- "You must know Richard that after finishing my studies and working for the hospital in Heidelberg I was looking for a way to become independent" he said while filling our glasses half with a Spaetlese from the region

- "You mean you wanted to start as a freelancer your own clinic" I said while reaching the glasses to the ladies and getting one for me

- "Exactly, Hindelang was among the potential candidates, not many, and after looking on the map I decided to apply for the job" he said and we clinked glasses

- "That's a good joke, don't tell me you didn't know where Hindelang was located" I said puzzled about his ingenuity

- "Of course I knew it was in Allgäu close to the Austrian border, but no more" he answered enjoying my perplexity

- "I see, the community was looking for an internist and you applied for the job just like that" I said still puzzled about his ingenuity

- "Right, and as I was the only candidate, the community offered me a favourable deal" he said that relishing each of his words

- "So it was a win-win situation for all partners" I concluded with some suspicion

- "I would say, it was a deal the Bavarian way which is very similar to the Texan way in the United States" Anton confirmed my supposition.

In December we spent Christmas together in Oberjoch and so forth during the whole year 1985. In 1986 I had a good overview of Frederike's income and financial construction and, so it was worth doing it, I decided to ask her to marry me during one of our triangular meetings, what she immediately wanted.

We set the wedding for 28 May 1986, a Wednesday and everything worked perfectly. After the wedding I had to take care of the formalities I needed, that means, I managed to convince her to create an offshore brass plate company to doctor our balances. The new company allowed, of course; each of us to have all rights and full access to all accounts of the company. A risky construction without the emergency exit I had up my sleeve and which already worked with Monika.

We had to clear with the banks, lawyers and tax consultant the legal and tax points emerging for this purpose. In this matter, there were, as usual, very many points to observe during the proceedings. We sold Frederike's houses to our offshore brass plate company to the lowest credible price to screw down tax and gave us ourselves a manager contract to protect our benefits and kept Frederike's apartment as company apartment. One more time, we didn't have to consider the Scottish inheritance law between spouses, it was better to let sleeping dogs lie.

Frederike also agreed on naming me beneficiary of her life insurance she already had.

Business as already seen!

Our relationship was a pure sexual affaire à trois twice a week as we had agreed. The only breaks I had were the hiking tours twice a week, my day off, Wednesday, the weekends with Anton and my journeys to Edinburgh and some journeys to Munich Frederike did normally alone. I knew I couldn't keep pace with the ladies for long. I had to find a solution, quickly, I had no choice. So I planned to clear the cat in September 1986 and make sure to have an alibi. I decided to give her the shot the night I departed on 15 September 1986, a Monday, to Edinburgh for a regular meeting, changing syringes before leaving and making sure the shot had worked. She was going to be alone at home during the whole night letting the shot come completely into effect and going to be found next morning by Aurelia and the cleaning woman.

As expected, following morning, Aurelia called me at the meeting and gave me the bad news. I told her to call Anton and wait until I come back. I gave the news to the funeral home in Hindelang I had already selected and said the doctor was on his way; they should wait for the doctor at my house. I was going to take the next flight to Munich where I always parked my car. In the meantime Anton arrived and examined Frederike's body and decided the cause of death was heart failure and signed the death certificate. Then the people from the funeral home took care of the body, transported and prepared it for cremation. No more body, no evidences.

Before the burial I managed to bring all valuable values to the apartment in Munich and contracted a household clearance company for doing the necessary clearance after my departure.

After the burial, I had the usual procedure; I cleared all legal matters with the banks, lawyers and tax consultant, let them do all necessary name rearrangements in the financial construction and hoped to overcome the ceremonies at the cemetery and find an unsuspicious way to have an orderly retreat from Aurelia. I wanted to come back to my real life with standard meetings… I wanted my healthy life back, I had to get over it. The "Leichenschmaus" was this time just for us three and the cleaning woman and took place in a depressive and sadden mood for all of us.

Next morning Aurelia came to my place and we talked:

- "Aurelia I am sure you understand that right now I am not able to switch off. I want to try to explain all those apparently contradictory feelings and behaviours I have in my inside. Frederike is a big loss for me and surely for you too, that's why I suggest that we first get over it" I said what I had prepared

- "My wording Richard... I feel awful and couldn't sleep at all last night... I know Frederike left footprints in your life too, I understand it of course, and the story is so moving and unique!" she said with emotion

- "And we met because of that strong link between you and Frederike!" I said with thick voice

- "... But, as the tragedy of her death is still near..." she replied with a real husky voice

- "Frederike was your first corpse I think" I added after a while

- "Indeed, I never thought that could be so hard to overcome, I feel uncomfortable, there are footprints for me too, which affect me deeply in my relationship with you" she said with tears in her eyes

- "I am not sure about the right wording; I just want to tell you that we should now keep distance from each other at least for a while" I said glad to have found the right words

- "Exactly what I was thinking of, the time is right now rough and unpleasant; the 'betrayal feeling' remains, though it has not any logic..." she said thankful for my wording

- "The memory is too vivid to flirt and charm each other" I stressed our thoughts

- "We should keep the link and not necessarily change our mind after our torrid loss" she added with husky voice again

- "You know you both were my sugar ladies bringing care, humour, culture and pleasures into my life, but that's why you and Frederike are indivisible in my mind" I said trying to reach my goal

- "I am sorry that our mostly rich and trustful relationship must be suspended now, but you are right, the memory of Frederike is still so vivid in our doing that we cannot go back to business as usual. We have to consider all those questionings" she stressed the thought again

- "To be or not to be, that is the question, you know..." I assisted her

- "All those moves forwards and backwards..." she confirmed

- "I won't disturb you any more; it is up to you to contact me any time you want. Every message I receive from you will be answered" I continued on the way to my goal

- "We agree on all these points, we now have to find a credible and unsuspicious way to explain our decision to Anton, to sugar the pill for him" she said convinced of her thought

- "I'll say that undeferrable businesses demand my presence in Edinburgh for the next months. I'll suggest that we spend the weekend together before I leave on Monday" I suggested

- "That's a good idea, we play golf and table tennis a last time and do the cooking together" she accepted with great relief.

We came together one more time on the weekend and I was glad I was given the opportunity to orderly retreat after finishing work. Anton still couldn't believe that Frederike had died that fast, he was certainly shocked though he was used in his profession to deal with death:

- "I still cannot believe that Frederike died" Anton said thrilled
- "We all three still cannot believe it" Frederike added stormy
- "It is a great loss for me and for you too, everything seemed so easy with her" I said not knowing how to lead the talk to my aim
- "Well, Richard what are your plans now?" Anton fortunately asked
- "I have just blank in my mind, but on the other hand I am grateful to have undeferrable businesses to do in Edinburgh for the next months, so I won't have time to think about Frederike during the day. Nights may be different, but that's something I must overcome by myself" I said with the necessary maturity in my voice
- "I understand you perfectly and think it's the best for you though your company in this remote spot was balm for my soul" Anton explained his actual mood
- "I don't know when we'll meet again; right now it is too early to say a word about that. When I see you both Frederike comes involuntarily to my mind and that hurts my soul, so forgive me if it takes its time for me to recover, but be sure, I'll let you know when I am ready to see you again" I stated in an adequate manner
- "It's the same with me, I don't know how long it will take to overcome this mood" Aurelia added with a voice still full of emotion
- "Frederike was a special friend and I'll keep her in my special memory" said Anton with thick voice and we finished the talk after a moment of silence.

On Monday I contacted a real estate agent in Hindelang to tell him my lawyers were going to contact him for the further procedure concerning the house sale in Oberjoch. I also told him the household clearance was already ordered and left afterwards Oberjoch to Edinburgh very satisfied with the leave-taking performance at Anton's place. It was time for me to recover from the exhausting life I had with the Bavarian sex-bombs. Oh what a relief it was! Peaceful mornings, peaceful noons, peaceful afternoons, peaceful evenings, peaceful nights... I was breathing normally... At that moment I thought let bygones be bygones...

I had to prepare my next chase, knowing that there is no one-size-fits-all strategy to get in touch with the desired person. Siloé was going to be my next cat and I hoped she was going to contact me in the near future because she always wrote from time to time.

Chapter 6

Siloé Barré

Siloé just finished her work and made a short break watching the majestic landscapes of the mountains around from the windows of her apartment in Chambéry as she decided to write me a letter to my address in Edinburgh. As it was November 1986, and according to her mood at that moment she also wrote some lines in French to wish:
- "Bonne année pour toi et ta famille, bonne santé aussi et beaucoup d'activités intéressantes de toutes sortes.
Amicalement"

I could read behind the lines, she wanted to meet me and I thought she was going to be my next cat. After interchanging a few letters, we decided to meet at her place in May 1987.

Chambéry was a nice charming town, similar to Heidelberg, site in Department de la Savoie, region Rhône-Alpes with about 60,000 inhabitants. The town had always been of importance for the transalpine road between Lyon and Turin and also had a very well-known university. Streets and places with lot of history, as well as the place with the four elephants, called elephants' fountain or affectionately by locals the 'four buttless', which at first glance during my first sightseeing in town I already associated to Siloé.

Her apartment was located in the Rue des Ècoles, near Parc du Verney, within walking distance from the train station. Everything in the apartment was standard in a standard French building of that time, only the windows were high-tech. The apartment had 3 bedrooms, one home office, living room, kitchen with a lot of closets, bathrooms, toilets and the classical multipurpose French balcony with garbage chute. The furniture was antique rustic in handcrafted cedar, something not common in France but her preference. By clear weather the 'Nivolet Cross' in the 'massif des Bauges', a magnificent view, could be seen from the kitchen barré and Mount Granier, the NE limit of the 'massif de la Chartreuse, from the living room, a site with history like almost any place in town as I already pointed out.

At our first meeting she showed me the city with the already mentioned elephants' fountain:

- "Here you see the famous elephants' place, four elephants without backside" Siloé said in an innocent tone

- "I understand" I said, but I really didn't understand why the elephants had no backside. They were placed looking at four different directions, the sculptures showing only approx. 1/3 of each elephant in relief, that is to say: emerging from the block the whole head until behind first forelegs. Siloé had a nice not missing butt I found very attractive. So I decided to identify her with the missing butts of the elephants...

She cut my deep reflections saying:

- "Did you know that Jean-Jacques Rousseau wrote the Declaration of the Rights of Man, the French version of the Bill of Rights, while living in Chambéry?"

- "Of course I did not" I said still thinking of the elephants as she continued her lecture:

- "The fountain was made by Victor Sappey in front of the castle in 1838"

- "Interesting" was my smart remark while she continued

- "This building commemorates the exploits of the Marathas in India led by General-Count de Boigne from 1751 to 1830"

- "For me it is a fountain composed of three parts" I added as singing in the rain

- "Good boy, the first represents four elephants without buttocks. The second is a column-shaped palm and the last is a statue of Count Boigne, dressed in his uniform" she finished as we left the place.

Later we did a lot of hiking in the Valley de la Tarentaise via Albertville and Le Meiller, a corner I suggested and which she didn't know that well and of course around Lac du Bourget, the largest natural lake in France.

At our tour through the Valley de la Tarentaise and Le Meiller she pointed out:

- "In spite of appearance and my fear before meeting you, I feel secure at your side"

- "I think it is because you only want quality on your road" I stressed trying to look innocent

- "Oh, how unpretentious" she replied teasing me

- "From my early childhood on I have been always very modest" I explained in my best self-confident tone

- "Knock it off, nasty boy. At the beginning as you were driving I was cautious and somehow under tension..." she added letting me feel her stimulation in her voice
- "And now I think you are relaxed and enjoying the tour" I said looking at her lap
- "It is true that I felt ill at ease at first in the car, but as you let me guide our way although you'd probably planned how to get there, I liked your relaxed way and I then felt at ease" she said in an inviting tone
- "I knew you were going to enjoy guiding us" I replied in the same tone
- "Indeed I enjoyed it. It was nice pointing at spots along the road: vineyards, rocks, mansions..." she said trying to sound relaxed
- "Sharing what you like in Savoy..." I said using polysemantic words
- "When I indicated the wrong way to col de la Madeleine, you didn't complain. You just turned around to follow indications shown on the map I finally took off my bag" she replied in the same tone
- "Easy going and the big easy" I said, feeling I had found the right approach to her.

We started meeting from time to time doing things the way she wanted: that meant we wouldn't have real sex before marrying, I still don't know why, but she however accepted to have all other kinds of sex with me. In her eyes, petting, fellatio and anal sex were not sex. I respected her decision not to have traditional sex with me though we did have sex in that special and delicious way. I had the impression she liked the pleasures I was allowed to give her with her apartment shutters always closed...What a funny lady!

Frequently, she abruptly said things I couldn't really understand. Her trains of thoughts without context were highly peculiar. One time for instance she said:
- "The moments at our encounter manage us to overcome such risks or temptations of making a seism of what we do" while I was stroking softly her tits, what she liked very much. Well, she had a lot of preferences like having anal sex and afterwards swallowing my sperm.

We decided to explore the surroundings when the weather conditions were steady:

The first tour took us to Annecy, capital of Haute-Savoie and the 'Pearl of French Alps', on the northern tip of its lake. The city is also known as Venice of the Alps: it has two canals and the river Thiou, which all of them turn and twist through the old city: a nice spot for large walks. We did both ways in town and around the lake. We had lunch-break on a bench at the one canal in the park and enjoyed the fresh air.

The next tour was Aix les Bains, Department de la Savoie in the Rhône-Alpes region, and the Lac du Bourget. The town is located on the eastern shore of the lake du Bourget. This was and still is a place for wealthy people and has, of course, a casino and a marina besides the well-known thermal baths, not the best place for hiking tours. We decided to go to the Dent du Chat for hiking, a decision not to repent of.

The third tour was Arith, a commune in the Department de la Savoie in the Rhône-Alpes region with a lot of ways to go and a hidden nice pond, she called lake, where we had our lunch-break sitting on rocks we covered with plastic bags she had packed with wise foresight, well, she knew the place well.

But we also did the Park of Birds, in French: parc des oiseaux, in Villars-Les-Dombes in the Department de l'Ain, one of the oldest ornithological parks in France, a nice place to watch birds and to make her feel confident.

But we also did other landmarks like the Croix du Nivolet above Chambéry, Mont Margeriaz in the Bauges, St Christophe de Couz, Mont Granier a high cliff limestone mountain with its north face overlooking Chambéry, cirque de Saint Même natural amphitheatre in the massif de la Chartreusse, Le Guiers Vif river, Fort Châtel, etc.

I was sure the time we shared was going to remain strongly rooted in her mind, well, I hoped. Somehow, we were led to a certain unity anyone of us could claim for. She was every time very tired after I left, maybe because there was just so much, so strong to experience in such a short time. She was in the mood of willing not to miss somewhat or someone important or not... all that she hadn't indulged herself for years. She was just being what she was in her wholeness, conscious of anything, accepting to extirpate elements from the very bottom of her mind. Although I saw in her eyes a let do, a choice protecting from getting too close. I was sure I had given her a very special opportunity in life.

After a while I found out that she was a wealthy lady descending from a well known French family of sausage manufacturers originally located in the region between Valence and Bergerac, but also with connections to Clermont-Ferrand and Auvergne. At the present she was the only alive in her family branch. The finances were managed by means of a complicated interlocked construction of several limited companies not easy to overview but well built to avoid excessive tax.

We were doing well and had at that time the calm to enjoy the beautiful landscapes around her place. One day, we were just walking around in Ardéche and she said after we came back to her place:
- "Richard, you cannot imagine my days of nightmare during the past years without you" she whispered with seducing voice
- "I probably don't but you can put your head on my shoulder" I said stroking her best parts
- "Oui, on connaît la chanson..." she added in trance
- "I only dream of traffic jams" I added challenging her
- "Come on, Richard. Behave and be serious!" she implored like a little child
- "Of course I am serious. Yesterday was a busy and fulfilling day I would say" I continued challenging her
- "I have now very, very, very warm thoughts..." she added with great expectation
- "The same warm thought I have?" I asked guiding her hand to my best part
- "Take it for granted. This parenthesis is really enchanting and brings me to a woman's life. Please, 'babe' me..." she said softly stroking my best part
- "If you insist..." I said driving my finger into her back door
- "I haven't been 'babed' since the Stone Age; how sweet it is to feel you!" she said melting my finger in her back door.

After getting a detailed overview of her finances and finding out how to get into her complicated construction I decided to do the next step and asked her to marry me, what she was willing to do. Before marriage we had to decide where we were going to reside so I told her:
- "I suppose we are going to reside here in Chambéry, aren't we?" I asked sure of getting the answer I was waiting for
- "If you don't mind that's what I would prefer" she quickly confirmed
- "That is alright for me, but you know I have every month business to do out of town; it is up to you if you want to accompany me during my journeys" I said just for the file because I really didn't want her to travel with me to Edinburgh
- "Thank you for asking, but in this respect I would prefer to stay in Chambéry if you don't mind" she said while holding two standard glasses with an asking glance
- "I see, I suppose it is due to the memories linked to Sarah and Edinburgh, which I completely understand and respect" I gave her a nod looking at the red wine carafe on the sideboard

- "That is correct, for me Edinburgh is strongly connected to Sarah" she said filling our glasses with a tasty wine of the region we drank in short sips while making love her way.

So that point was all set. What Siloé didn't know was that I also had married and cleared Monika and Frederike and I wasn't going to tell her anything about that.

We set 17 November 1987 for the marriage in Chambéry due to legal requirements to arrange a marriage in France. We had to apply a month in advance to the town hall where we normally lived, in our case Chambéry. There were again so many points to be observed, that we decided to let the lawyers and notaries do the work for us and gave them the required powers to act in our name for the marriage application. The 40 days of residence, 30 days' residence plus ten days for publication of the banns and the witnesses were no problem. The other documents like passports, residence registration, birth certificates, and for me as a widowed person the death certificate of my wife, and a recent medical certificate were reached in legalised copy with all corresponding translations. A lot of papers! But we were then issued with the pre-marital certificate, so our notification of our impending wedding, the banns, could be published ten days before the ceremony at the town hall where the wedding was to take place, in our case as I already pointed out Chambéry.

The marriage ceremony was very simple and afterward we had a short reception with our witnesses to our wedding, namely her cleaning woman and her husband, before leaving for our honeymoon, one week in Deauville, a commune in Department Calvados, Normandy region, and well-known as the queen of the Norman beaches. The Flowery Coast region is still home to French high society and a fashionable holiday resort for the international upper class, a nice spot to spend a few days and a lot of money.

The nights of our honeymoon were of pure vaginal sex with a very hungry lady intending to clear her evident backlog and scarce sleep for both of us.

After our return to Chambéry I was able to give her pleasures without exaggeration.

As we were subjected to a communal regime I managed to get unsuspicious all necessary powers for unlimited access to her finances. I also suggested to close a life insurance for her with a coverage amount of half a million dollars, death benefits tax-free, and with me as the sole beneficiary. That meant I was all set for the next step for clearing the cat. Well, I had every month business to do out of town, which meant that I was, as agreed, usually one week each month on journey. I thought September would be a good month to clear the cat. Until then we had a 'normal' life for the neighbours and stayed mostly at Chambéry, participating from time to time in golf tournaments and in hiking tours as part of social life.

One more point in my plan was to have a physician at hand: one of our golf partners was Geoffroy Prost, a physician in general medicine in town, whom I asked to become our family physician during a golf play, something not really usual in France, but primordial for my injecting goals. I had no hesitation about my plan and had enough time to let it come into effect:

- "Geoffroy, do you mind to become our family physician?" I asked him as we were on the teeing ground during play on hole 5

- "Not at all; it is just not usual in France to go to the doctor for prophylaxis, that means before one needs a doctor, just for prevention" he said choosing one club to tee off

- "Well, it is just that we may consider family planning in the near future" I said while we were walking to the balls

- "That's a good idea. You are welcome any time. Make appointments as opportune in my clinic. I'll tell my secretary that you will call. So it won't be a problem" he said pointing at his ball

- "Indeed, I mostly want to check Siloé's diabetes, but that is something we can discuss at your place" I said giving him a nod and waiting for his next hit

- "Oh, I didn't know she has diabetes and you are right, for family planning this is an important matter" he said after hitting the ball and we closed the topic.

On the following day I was just thinking of the absurdity of life and the meaning of choices. I was missing for a moment my youthful tiger shape. This was for me a moment of very heavy melancholy I had to overcome quickly... Stress was growing and growing, my night was full of existential questions. I went for a walk early in the morning and it did good to walk on the endless and empty streets of the town. During the walk I realized I was not the rock of Gibraltar and I was in spirit with Stella, Fatema and our unborn child. I had to let my plan concerning Siloé come into effect. Time has a new dimension when the basic rhythms are upside down.

In this mood, I took into consideration the different logics of male and female: males simply have an on/off switch and females a lot of complicated dashboards... which was very funny for me and somehow caricatured. And sometimes being a no answer an answer... females are not simple at all. Now I am just trying to explain all those apparently contradictory feelings and behaviours... I know Stella and Fatema left footprints in my life, I understand it of course, and the story is so moving and unique! And I met Siloé because of that strong link between me and the poison! But, as the tragedy of Fatema's death is still near, there are strong footprints for me, which affect me deeply, especially in my relationship with Siloé... The well-known 'betrayal feeling' remains, though it has no logic... I want to eat the cat and simultaneously clear the cat, something like eat the cake and have it, and this will happen in the near future as already planned. The whole remembrance of this deep and eternal love to Stella and Fatema brings back to the surface the strong reservations I had about physical love, Siloé's motivation was a different one, but the end result was the same as I remember... Then leaving for a certain time, it was like a sailor's life... I'll be delighted to clear the cat but I have to consider all those questionings, to be or not to be, that is the question, those moves forwards and backwards... They do mean that life isn't that univocal... It seems too complicated...

Then I made an appointment for the following week and everything worked perfectly. We became Geoffroy's patients and that was the point I wanted to score. According to the check-up we were both healthy and Siloé's sugar values were correct. Her congenital heart defect was detected for the file, but the anomaly was medical within normal limits and Geoffroy said no treatment was necessary. As the weather was still gorgeous I suggested making a small tour to Arith which we enjoyed very much.

December 1987 we spent together in Chambéry in a frame of boring routine for me because our relationship degenerated into a pure sexual relationship. The only breaks I had were my stays in Edinburgh.

I knew redemption was coming closer and closer, so I just had to keep pace with her for a few months. I had to wait for C-day for the solution, the access to peace in my mind, I had no choice. So I had to make sure to have an alibi. I decided to give her the shot the night I departed to Edinburgh via Paris on 12-13 September 1988, a Monday-Tuesday, for a regular business journey, as I already had decided months ago. Before leaving I changed syringes and made sure the shot had begun to be effective. She was going to be alone at home during the whole night and the shot was going to come completely into effect. Next morning, she was going to be found by the cleaning woman and I was going to be miles away.

As expected, following morning, the cleaning woman called me at home in Edinburgh and gave me the bad news. I told her to call Dr. Prost and wait until I came back. I contacted the funeral home I already had in mind and gave the news saying the doctor was on his way; they should wait for the doctor at my house. I was going to take the next flight to Geneva and take this time the shuttle bus to Chambéry.

Geoffroy arrived and examined Siloé's body and decided the cause of death was heart failure and signed the death certificate. Then the body was immediately transported and prepared for cremation as I have ordered. No more body, no more evidences.

After the burial, I had the same procedure as usual; I cleared all legal matters with the banks, lawyers and tax consultant, and let them do all necessary name rearrangements and sales in the financial construction. After putting my affairs in order I took my paraphernalia and returned finally to Edinburgh. What a relief it was, I was back to my real life with great desires to find the next cat to clear.

Katarina was supposed to be my next cat, located in Spain, owning two hotels and been a Polish descendant girl with a strong catholic background.

Chapter 7

Katarina Ramakow

Checking the correspondence after my return to Edinburgh in October 1988 I found two letters from Katarina. The first one was business as usual, but in the second one she wrote: "It would be great to meet you again after such a long time. Let me know if you would like to come to Rosas, you know you are welcome any time", and as she was my next candidate before running out of cats, I decided to gently intensify our contact as she sent me that open invitation. It did fit in with my plans, so I called her that very evening:

- "Hi Katarina, here is Richard speaking..." I said testing the water

- "Hi Richard glad to hear you" she said in a clear and trustfully tone

- "I just came back home and read your letters. After checking my agenda I have two meeting options for us: next month or May 1989, because I think that you will spend Christmas with your tribe in Poland" I said sure to have left all fire exits open

- "Indeed I already set up with my tribe our Christmas program and May seems to me too far away, so why don't you come to my place in November?" was her straight response leaving me flabbergasted

- "Well, no choice, we meet in November. Now forgive me please, but I have no idea how to get there" I said after recovering

- "To put the matter in a nutshell you have to fly to Barcelona and I would fetch you at the airport" she clearly stated

- "No please I don't want to incommode you, I could rent a car at the airport to get to your place" I said trying to appear considerately

- "That figures to you! Down-to-earth boy! You don't incommode me at all. It is just not easy to find the way out the first time. You should know that the traffic in Barcelona is chaotic 24 hours a day" she said teacherlike

- "Alright chief, your wish is my command" I said paying attention to her wording 'find the way out the first time' as a kind of gentle invitation for the future

- "Do you have already a concrete time-window for our meeting?" she asked coming to the point

- "I still have to re-check it once more and find out the fly itineraries, but I think 21 November is a good day" I said knowing exactly the time-window was free

- Great, I suggest you stay at my place from 21 until 28 November" she declared

- "That would fit like a glove for me. I confirm later the dates and let you know the flights I book and the landing time" I finished the call in a relaxed tone and satisfied of good score achieved.

Two days later, I called her again to confirm the dates and thought it would be the best to do what came naturally. I dedicated some time to get some information about the town: it was a municipality on the Spanish Costa Brava with approx. 15,000 inhabitants, situated on the coast at the northern end of the Gulf of Roses/Rosas; it was also an important fishing port and, of course, a location for well-heeled tourists. The town was connected to the world outside by means of the C260 via Figueres/Figueras, approx. 33km. That's what I told Katarina I knew about Rosas during our conversation from the airport to Rosas. She was pleased I had done some researches concerning the town:

- "Wonderful, you have an idea of the town, most people don't. Actually it is firstly a tourist center, but right now people had found some ruins which have to be scientifically analysed before evaluation and the municipality also plans to do some restoration work on the walls of the Ciutadella" she explained in the routine tone of someone who states this not for the first time to the audience

- "Enough sightseeing for tourist, now tell me how come that you reside here, at the end of the world?" I asked eager for knowledge

- "That's easy to answer: I have two hotels running in town" was her satisfied enigmatic answer to my query

- "Really, you are a hotel owner?" I asked pleased to hear the simple reason

- "Yes, and don't laugh because they are 4 and 5 stars hotels" she said in a challenging tone

- "Spanish stars I suppose..." I added teasing her

- "Well, real Spanish stars!" she stated seriously

- "Of course, I am sure the rooms aren't holes in the wall" I said trying to soothe her with a light malicious smile on my lips

- "Be sure of that... Oh no! You are just teasing me! I was taking in by you! Do penance, bad boy!" she said gladdened, laughing
- "I am not a bad boy, I am Denis the Menace, you know...".

At that time we had already arrived to her house at tea-time, coffee-time for Germans.

The house was located up one hill of Rosas with a panoramic view, butler, cook, house employees, and security guards, what she tried to qualify:

- "Don't be surprised about all this jazz because it is the usual way in Spain"
- "I suppose all due to security reasons" I said thinking this was paradise for me
- "Right, wealthy people must be careful in this matter and that's why I can do all that with tax reductions..." she added in a businesslike tone
- "You have a resident status in Spain, is there any prerequisite for getting the status?" I asked incidentally
- "First of all, you have to be registered in Spain for at least five years" she said again businesslike

This was a bad point I had to keep in mind for the future. After tea-time we went for a walk to the marina and kept talking and talking and talking. At 21:00h we had a delicious dinner and continued talking and talking and talking until we went to bed together. Next morning she woke up in a very sweet mood and I was satisfied with my doing.

At lunch I told her that I had some businesses to do in France on Thursday and asked if I could have her car for the day. Meanwhile we had a very good time together.

On Thursday I took the car and drove to France, not for businesses but to visit the place where Stella had her car accident years ago. It was a very emotional moment for me and I felt very close to Stella, Fatema and junior.

Later at Katarina's place I was the same as ever and could give her much pleasure and enchanting conversation. She told me we were going to make us dinner on Friday evening in a good restaurant, well; it was one of the world best and famous restaurants at that time. That was a wonderful experience for me and the night was again unforgettable for her. During the remaining days I did my best and could keep her highly satisfied and I decided to meet her again at my place at the end of January.

After our long talks I knew she had first worked as a translator for the European Community in Brussels and Strasbourg, with the usual tax free benefits, had quitted the job and bought the two hotels and the house in Rosas in a good bargain; well, she went from strength to strength. She was a self-made millionaire with some relatives in Poland she did not visit frequently in the past, due to the iron curtain:

- "You know now the political situation is changing and I am refreshing family links" she said

- "Yes, the political landscape is radically changing in Europe, what are your plans concerning Poland?" I asked in passing

- "My deeply loved 98 years old uncle lives in Wieliczka, his name is Adalbert, but we call him just Adi and his wife is Magdalena" she said in a sweet childish mood

- "Adi is a peculiar nickname, I like it" I said showing great interest

- "I am going to visit him and some other relatives for Christmas" she said waiting for my reaction

- "I see, how you would get there?" I asked again in passing

- "The best option will be to fly from Barcelona to Kraków because Wieliczka is located in the Kraków metropolitan area, only approx. 10km southeast from Kraków and then rent a car. I will spend 12 days there and hope to be back for Epiphany" she said looking at me with certain expectation.

I thought that would be great because it was going to fit in with my plans to invite her for late January to Edinburgh, so I asked her:

- "What do you think of coming to my place at the end of January?"

- "You knew I was waiting for that question! I would be delighted to be there for a week if it is alright for you..." she said relieved to hear that

- "It's a deal!" I finished the conversation.

I also got an overview of her financial construction which was lousy and urgently needed a serious remodelling. That was going to be my next task after marrying her.

Before our next meeting I studied the Spanish laws, especially the chapter concerning the inheritance tax for non residents. After having it double checked with my lawyers I knew a wedding according to Spanish law was no option for my plans: too much trouble because with less than five years of residence in Spain I only could be considered a non-resident and therefore governed by the Spanish state standard of the inheritance tax, which was extremely unfavourable for me. I therefore decided to invite her to officially reside in Edinburgh until the wedding was over. In this case the friendly Scot family law would apply. I told the lawyers to prepare everything and stand by.

Time went by very fast and we met again in January. I fetched her at the airport and Katarina had a good impression of my hut:
- "The floor on the garage is new, isn't it?" she asked knowing she was right
- "Yes, I needed room for James and Mary and that's why the outbuilding was necessary" I said completely sure that James and Mary were going to observe my orders not to say a word about the past
- "It fits perfectly with the house" she said with great satisfaction
- "I am glad you like it" I said and we kept talking and talking and talking as usual.
That time we did all sightseeing in town, also the murder tour, which she enjoyed very much:
- "I think this night tour through town is something for people like uncle Adi"
- "Who knows..." I said keeping in mind this point for later use on request.
We had a good time and she left Edinburgh in a cheerful mood.
At our following meeting in February we decided to get civil married in Edinburgh and she also agreed on officially registering her residence at my place. We were all set and I let the lawyers do their work. In March we were ready for the wedding and fixed the day on 25 April 1989.
She accepted that I didn't want a church marriage, but she didn't know my real reason: I knew that in such a case all relatives were going to come or worst, we had to go to Poland to celebrate a church wedding. That's why I suggested we marry in Edinburgh, civil as planned, with her uncle Adi and wife Magdalena as witnesses, and go later to Wieliczka to post-celebrate our wedding with the other relatives.
My suggestion was immediately accepted and Katarina started preparing the event. In such occasions family becomes very, very, very large. She found an events restaurant in the same town of Wieliczka with a lot of facilities and an appropriate time-window for us.
We married in Edinburgh on 25 April 1989, had a lot of fun with her uncle and his wife. They both spoke very good German but not good English, so kept talking in German. Due to Magdalena's leg problems, she was only 92 years old, as Adi kept saying, we did most sightseeing motorised, excepting the night tour which we did walking, well we had to do on foot and Magdalena survived it easily. It was a great experience for both of them. On the other hand, my great experience was that I didn't know old people could drink the vodka

quantities they did. As we left to Wieliczka my bar was run out of vodka. We post-celebrated the wedding as planned in Poland on 2-3 May with open-end until next midnight. It was a nice party and Katarina's uncle Adi and Magdalena were nice persons and very happy to be with us and to have a very good excuse to drink some more vodka. Katarina loved teasing him and his wife. On the other hand, he gave me some history lessons about Wieliczka: the town was founded by Duke Premislas II of Poland and had one of the world's oldest operating salt mines.

In June I convinced Katarina of the advantages of my financial construction of offshore brass plate companies. Her hotels and house were sold to one of my mail-drop corporations in Guernsey and she received a proportional share in the financial construction. In case of her death Scot law was favourable for me as I already knew.

I planned to clear the cat in March 1990 in Rosas because she already had a very handy doctor there taking care of the hotel guests, the cemetery had a crematorium and there was no sophisticated crime investigation department in town. Meanwhile, she enjoyed her time with me staying alternatively in Rosas and Edinburgh.

As March came closer, I had to clear the cat and make sure to have an alibi. I decided to give her the shot on the night of 25-26 March when I departed to Edinburgh, changing syringes before leaving and making sure the shot had worked. She was going to be alone at home during the whole night letting the shot come into effect and going to be found next morning by the cleaning woman.

Following morning, the butler called me at Edinburgh and gave me the bad news. I told him to call the doctor and wait until I came back. I gave the news to the funeral home and said the doctor was on his way; they should wait for the doctor at the house. The doctor arrived and examined Katarina's body and decided the cause of death was heart failure and signed the death certificate. Then the body was transported and prepared for cremation.

I gave Adi a ring to tell him what had happened and that Katarina was going to be buried in Spain:

- "Thank you so much for calling; it comes indeed as a shock to us" Adi said with evidently difficulty to articulate

- "Do you think you would be able to attend the ceremonies?" I asked knowing he was not going to assist to the burial

- "No, forgive us but that would be too much for us, but I promise to order a mass for Katarina's dead" he said and Magdalena added from the side:

- "We are both deeply shaken by the news about Katarina's death, I still cannot believe it; it comes as a shock to us"

- "I understand perfectly. I would like to visit you at the end of April in Wieliczka if it is alright for you" I frankly suggested
- "Yes, please come, that would be balm for our souls" Adi said with husky voice
- "I can fly to Kraków on 24 April and stay two nights" I specified the date
- "Very good, I already marked it red in my agenda" Adi said with great relief and Magdalena added:
- "We wait for you with great expectation"
- "See you then" I concluded glad to have fulfilled my duty.

After the burial, I had the same procedure as every time without a hitch and departed to Edinburgh as planned. After my return, I cleared all legal matters with the bank, lawyers and tax consultant and couldn't believe I was run out of cats...

In late April I visited Adi and Magdalena as scheduled. It was a difficult duty for me towards them, but they were very grateful for the visit and I could finally close that chapter.

Epilog

Back home, I had the usual daily routine and on the evening of 24 May 1990, a Thursday, I received a phone call from a desperate Aurelia:
- "Sorry to disturb you, but I don't know what to do..." she said trembling with fear in her voice
- "Easy Aurelia, what is going on?" I asked trying to calm her
- "Bad news concerning Anton" she said stumbling
- "Tell me what did happen?" I insisted on getting the details
- "A cerebrovascular accident occurred to him in the night to Monday" she finally said a sentence I could understand
- "You mean the blood supply to part of his brain was interrupted or severely reduced. When and how did you notice this?" I asked for more details
- "Yes, brain tissue was deprived of oxygen and food, as the emergency doctor told me later. Anton noticed something was wrong with him at the time he wanted to stand up from bed at the usual time" she said getting a little relaxed
- "That means, he was conscious" I enquired
- "Yes, but he could not move, he had developed at that time a sudden paralysis on the left side of his body" she said breathing heavily
- "Was he able to articulate in a normal way?" was my next question
- "Well, not in a normal way, but I could understand him and he told me to dial emergency, which I immediately did" she said still breathing heavily
- "I think the doctor came and ordered Anton's transport to the nearest hospital" I tried to help her saying what is usually done in such cases as I learned in an emergency course years ago
- "Right, they prepared him for transport to Sonthofen with a Ringer's solution" she said proud of still knowing what the emergency team did

- "Standard procedure, did they already add some anticoagulant?" I asked feeling she was then coming down to calm

- "No, that came later, at the hospital in Sonthofen, some antithrombotic agents, as I have been told" she said with a lost voice

- "And where are you now?" was my next question

- "Now we are in Munich at the university hospital and doctors concentrate on getting the right diagnosis, that is to say, is it a ischemic stroke, caused by blockage of a blood vessel, or a hemorrhagic stroke, caused by bleeding into the brain or into the space surrounding the brain" she said with a medical touch in her voice

- "Very good, Munich is the right place for him. Are you right now staying in a hotel?" I tried to calm her again

- "No, right now I follow up on the diagnosis at the hospital, but I booked already for tonight at a hotel" she answered like brave girls use to do

- "First thing you do tomorrow morning is to go to my house in Schwabing and get the keys for my apartment from the janitor, Mr. Micha. I'll inform him after we finish. Then you go to the apartment and turn on the refrigerator and freezer; check also that doors of both are closed. Do you want me to come to Munich tomorrow evening?" I asked anticipating

- "I didn't dare ask you to come, but I would feel much better if you could arrange it. I could buy some victuals and prepare dinner for us" she said glad to think of standard matters

- "Feel free to do so; buy some tea too and all the usual stuff because the apartment is food wise empty. Alright, I inform the janitor now and see you tomorrow evening at my place" I said feeling she was grateful for my help

- "Thank you and see you tomorrow" she before getting off the phone.

I immediately informed Mr. Micha to clear the matter with the keys next morning:

- "Good evening Mr. Micha, Richard Pages speaking"

- "Good evening Mr. Pages; what can I do for you?" he said expecting my orders

- "Tomorrow morning Mrs. Aurelia Tiede will fetch my apartment keys and will stay in there for a while" I said businesslike

- "Yes, Mrs. Aurelia Tiede, Sir" he said taking note of it

- "I'll also arrive tomorrow evening" I added

- "Yes Sir!" he concluded.

I knew strokes are vital emergency and medical treatment is crucial for the patients because early actions minimize brain damages and potential complications. No wonder that Aurelia was lost and needed help and I wanted to help. I booked a flight for next day 16:00h to Munich and went to bed.

Next day I arrived at the apartment at 19:12h where Aurelia was waiting for me with dinner and a great urge to speak:

- "Richard, you don't know how much good you do to me. I told Anton you were coming and he was highly pleased to hear that"

- "Come on, I just do what I can. If he is pleased, it means that he is conscious. Did the hospital finally find out what is going on with him?" I asked while we took the plates and glasses to the table

- "He is conscious and stabilized. The hospital is still looking for the cause of the disorder, well they already discarded hemorrhagic stroke" she specified reaching me cutlery and napkins

- "Does he still have the paralysis" I asked for details setting the table

- "I regret to say yes" she gave the requested detail while cutting some bread I put in the bread-basket I brought to the table

- "I think it is right now irrelevant whether the blood supply to part of his brain occurs when the arteries to his brain became narrowed or blocked, causing severely reduced blood flow, in medical terms ischemia, or when a blood clot, in medical terms thrombus, formed in one of the arteries that supply blood to his brain" I said letting her take some salad

- "That's exactly what the doctors said. They treat him with antithrombotic agents. Anton thinks the clot may be caused by fatty deposits, a kind of plaque, he said, that build up in arteries and cause reduced blood flow, namely atherosclerosis, or other artery conditions" she said passing me the salad and some bread

- "What about numbness of the face, arm or leg" I said before starting eating the salad

- "Until a certain degree he has also developed sudden numbness and weakness on the left side of his body, besides the paralysis in his face, arms and legs. Similarly, the left side of his mouth droops when he tries to smile" she explained after we finished the salad

- "You know it's a serious matter with him" I said passing her potatoes, vegetables and meat

- "I know, but let's have dinner now though I don't feel like eating" she said in a bad mood

- "You must be strong and that means now you eat something with me" I said categorically while serving us some water

- "You are right, of course…" she said as she started eating

- "Don't think any further! Did you buy some food for tomorrow?" I said trying to divert her thoughts
- "Yes, Sir!" she answered in her best brave-girl manner
- "I think it is better if we sleep in the same bed" I said taking the used plates to the kitchen the way waiters use to do
- "That may help me to sleep a little because since Monday I haven't slept much, as you can imagine" she said serving the ice-cream in dessert bowls we took to the table
- "That's why I suggest this. At what time did you tell Anton we are coming tomorrow?" I asked after finishing the ice-cream
- "I told him we may drop in at 10 o'clock" she answered taking the bowls to the kitchen
- "That's a good time for us. We visit him, leave for lunch and go by car to Oberjoch to pick up what you both may need" I said while loading the dishwasher
- "Duds and cosmetic are urgently needed" she said putting some detergent in the dishwasher
- "You tell me which way you prefer to go to Oberjoch" I said pressing the dishwasher start button
- "I prefer A96 Munich-Memmingen, then A7 Memmingen-Kempten and finally B310 Kempten-Oberjoch. Distance is approx. 200 km i.e. 40km longer than the one via A96 and normal roads, but faster because it is almost only freeway. It takes 2 hours driving under normal traffic conditions" she said after we made the kitchen clear
- "That means we need tomorrow at least 5 hours for that" I said calculating after brushing my teeth
- "I want to get asleep in your arms" she said after brushing her teeth and getting into bed at my side
- "Night, night" I said and gave her a good night kiss.

Considering her swiftly snoring, she certainly was tired and got a recovering sleep. Next morning she was in a better mood and after breakfast we went shopping at the supermarket at the corner and put the whole stuff in the kitchen and refrigerator before leaving for the hospital. When we arrived there the 'visit' was over, but the doctor in charge came immediately in the room and we had the opportunity to talk with him in calm:
- "Richard, I am so glad to see you, let me introduce you my colleague, Professor Dr. Martin Schulze, who is taking care of me" Anton said with a frank welcoming smile on his face
- "Glad to met you Professor Dr. Schulze" I said while shaking hands with him
- "It's my pleasure Mr. Pages" he responded simultaneously

Then a straightforward talk developed concerning Anton's state. The doctors at the hospital still classified the stroke without an obvious explanation as cryptogenic, that's to say of unknown origin, and they couldn't sound the all-clear signal for his case. We had to wait and see how situation developed. Anton's paralysis had fortunately decreased a little, but was still there. Doctors hoped the treatment with antithrombotic agents would help, but they firstly were eager to find the cause. A lot of analyses were already done and more were coming. The three of us had the best impression concerning the hospital. After Dr. Schulze left we talked a lot and told Anton we were going after lunch to Oberjoch to fetch some duds and cosmetics and asked him if he wanted to have something concrete from there. Lunch is always served early in hospitals, so we left after helping him with the meal at 12 o'clock.

After lunch, I told Aurelia to drive the way down and I was going to drive back. We were lucky because the freeways A96 and A7 were not crowded and Aurelia drove most time 200-220km per hour. The last part of the way was the national road B310 and we had to observe the speed limits as brave citizens. The way back was the same and we were not too late back home. We had dinner and watched a thriller on TV while in bed and had a calm night.

Next morning, we went to the hospital after breakfast and brought duds and cosmetics and the other things Anton had requested. I told him I was flying back to Edinburgh on Sunday at 18:12h, and after rearranging my agenda I was coming again a bit earlier next Friday. The same time was to be scheduled as necessary for my next arrives on Fridays and departures on Sundays. Anton's lunch was brought in and we helped him with the meal. Then Aurelia and I had lunch at the cafeteria and came back to him. We left the hospital at 14:00h and Aurelia gave me later a ride to the airport.

That was our routine for the next 3 weeks. During that period we took into consideration the fact that, if everything worked perfectly, Anton was going to remain a person in need of nursing for the rest of his life.

Friday 15 June I arrived as usual after lunch and we went to the hospital. We found Anton in a bad mood because he had headaches. We consulted the nurse and Professor Dr. Schulze and decided to give him some sedatives and to keep him under observation. We left the hospital at 19:00h and had dinner at my home under high tension. The night was suboptimal for Aurelia. Saturday we went early to the hospital and Professor Dr. Schulze was already waiting for us:

- "Dear Mrs. Tiede, I am so glad you arrive on time, we already tried unsuccessfully to reach you on the phone: we have a problem, because your husband had a loss of consciousness last night, headache and vomiting because of increased intracranial pressure from leaking blood compressing the brain"
- "Does it mean emergency operation is indicated?" I asked straight ahead
- "Correct, it is a high risk operation because opening the cranial vault can increase the bleeding, but we have no choice. Your husband already agreed but we wanted to inform and ask you permission to proceed to the operation" Professor Dr. Schulze said in a very serious tone
- "In terms of intracerebral hemorrhages it is the only chance, so please proceed. May we see him now?" Aurelia asked businesslike
- "Yes Mrs. Tiede, we waited for you before starting. We give you half an hour, and then we begin preparing him for the operation" Professor Dr. Schulze said and led us to Anton's room.

We came in and saw Anton on his bed with a lot of instruments around him and conscious but under sedatives. He knew his chances were not high and that's what he told us and gave instructions accordingly just in case. I told him I was going to stay as long as necessary in Munich and left them alone for a while. Aurelia called me and I gave him a soft handshake and he said:
- "Man sieht sich!"
- "Man sieht sich" I answered trying to find an English equivalent for that German idiom; maybe 'see ya' or 'be seeing you' or 'see ya on the flipside', but who could care, equivocality is the spice of language.

Professor Dr. Schulze and his team explained later next morning that after opening the cranial vault the bleeding increased as feared, they tried to stop the bleeding by all means but too many blood vessels were bleeding and an ischemic cascade occurred, many cells died before the bleeding was stopped. Anton was then transported to the intensive station but there was no hope that he could recover consciousness again. Aurelia had to decide what to do and she told them what Anton had already determined for such a case.

It was Sunday, 17 June 1990, 08:25h when he passed away after being disconnected from the machines. I packed Anton's personal effects and notified the hospital station that the funeral home from Bad Hindelang was going to take care of Anton's corpse.

At home and on behalf of Aurelia, I called the funeral home and ordered what had to be done. I also told them that we were going to be there next day. We had a very grievous lunch and decided to leave to Oberjoch that very afternoon.

Aurelia drove as usual the way down; this time we had no hurry at all, she didn't drive faster than 150km per hour. Some convoys were also on the road, but we had no traffic jam. Driving was easy until we got to the bridge close to a hotel in Landsberg: there was a convoy on the way, composed of one bus, two trucks, one more bus, three more trucks and a car at the end. At the very time we were passing the bus in-between the bus lost control 20 meters ahead of us, crashed against the bridge pillar to the right, overturned, skidded to the left lane, crashed at the guardrail to the left, taking our car with it. The result was a huge accident with 9 vehicles involved and many casualties. Our car was complete destroyed and I had a funny feeling missing my own body... Everything looked normal, and Aurelia was at my side incessantly repeating

- "It was not my fault; it was not my fault..." while we were looking at our still warm bodies on the highway with numerous excoriations, deep indentations and cuts

- "Of course it was not your fault, Aurelia, take it easy... Do you know where we are now?" I said as a chorus behind me called:

- "Richard, we are behind you as usual"

- "Stella, Fatema, Junior, I am so glad to be with you again" I said while Aurelia kept asking:

- "What happens to us, what happens to me, what happens to us, what happens to me?"

- "Don't worry Aurelia, Anton is also behind you. Now we go different ways, you with Anton and we with Richard" the chorus answered

- "Man sieht sich" we all said and vanished leaving in the air the imprints of our baneful story.